Wedding Rows

Wedding Rows

Kate Kingsbury

WHEELER
CHIVERS

This Large Print edition is published by Wheeler Publishing, Waterville, Maine USA and by BBC Audiobooks Ltd, Bath, England.

Published in 2006 in the U.S. by arrangement with The Berkley Publishing Group, a division of Penguin Group (USA) Inc.

Published in 2006 in the U.K. by arrangement with the author.

U.S. Softcover   1-59722-241-0   (Cozy Mystery)
U.K. Hardcover 10: 1 4056 3812 5   (Chivers Large Print)
U.K. Hardcover 13: 978 1 405 63812 8
U.K. Softcover 10: 1 4056 3813 3   (Camden Large Print)
U.K. Softcover 13: 978 1 405 63813 5

The text of this Large Print edition is unabridged.
Other aspects of the book may vary from the original edition.

Set in 16 pt. Plantin by Ramona Watson.

Printed in the United States on permanent paper.

British Library Cataloguing-in-Publication Data available

Library of Congress Cataloging-in-Publication Data

Kingsbury, Kate.
    Wedding rows / by Kate Kingsbury.
        p. cm. — (Wheeler publishing large print cozy mystery)
    Originally published: New York : Berkley, 2006. (A Manor House mystery)
        ISBN 1-59722-241-0 (lg. print : sc : alk. paper)
    1. World War, 1939–1945 — England — Fiction.   2. Women detectives — England — Fiction.   3. Weddings — Fiction.
    4. Manors — Fiction.   5. England — Fiction.   6. Large type books.   I. Title.   II. Wheeler large print cozy mystery.
    PR9199.3.K44228W43 2006
        813′.54—dc22
                                                    2006007671

Wedding Rows

Chapter 1

Seated in the second row of the centuries-old church, Lady Elizabeth Hartleigh Compton folded her hands in her lap and gazed with satisfaction at the guests slowly filing into the narrow pews. There was something about a wedding that brought out the best in people.

Getting married in wartime presented a unique set of problems. On top of the usual flurry of preparations, there was the huge problem of securing gowns for the bride and her attendants. With clothes being on ration, finding enough coupons was daunting.

Once news of Priscilla Pierce's upcoming springtime nuptials to Captain Wally Carbunkle had spread throughout the village, however, some of the most surprising people came forward.

Rita Crumm, for instance, who coveted her belongings as zealously as a squirrel hoarding nuts, was the first to present Priscilla with five precious coupons. Lilly, her daughter, followed soon after, though Elizabeth suspected that the young girl had responded to a certain amount of wrathful pressure from her mother.

One by one the offers had drifted in. Priscilla had given Elizabeth a full and tearful accounting during a visit to Wally's cottage shortly before the much-anticipated invitations were sent out.

According to the prospective and exceedingly nervous bride, Bessie from the Bake Shop had offered to make the wedding cake, with donations of egg rations from her staff.

Following Rita Crumm's example, or more likely her orders, the members of the Housewives League each pledged to bring food for the reception, to be held in the village hall. Florrie Evans, who turned out to be an adept seamstress, worked day and night to sew gowns not only for the bride, but also for the maid of honor and two bridesmaids.

Elizabeth herself had donated flowers from her gardens, while Earl Monroe, the American AAF major billeted in her mansion, offered to scrounge a silk parachute from the base for the wedding gown.

Priscilla and Wally issued an invitation to everyone who had contributed, and right now the tiny church seemed to be bursting at the seams. The vicar, Elizabeth reflected, would be most pleased to have such a bountiful attendance for a change.

Having given up most of her own coupons, she had elected to wear an elegant peach silk gown for the occasion. It had been in her possession for several years but was seldom worn. Her peaches-and-cream hat and gloves were new, but she'd made do with a pair of cream shoes that Desmond, her gardener and jack-of-all-trades, had made presentable by repairing the heels.

Seated next to her on the slim bench, Major Earl Monroe looked resplendent in his uniform. Elizabeth was hard put not to keep staring at him. She'd been afraid he might not be able to attend the wedding. For the last few weeks his absences had grown more frequent. Although he hadn't admitted as much, Elizabeth knew he was flying missions over France and Germany. Dangerous missions that, according to reports in the newspaper, were taking a toll on the airplanes and the courageous men who flew in them.

The sight of him these days brought a small measure of relief, only to be replaced by terror every time he said good-bye again. She had learned to put her fear on hold while she was with him and concentrate instead in making the most of every second in his company.

Each time they met, the moment she set eyes on him she wanted to melt into his arms. Definitely unbecoming for the lady of the manor and quite out of the question. Then again, a lot of what went on in her mind was most unfitting for her position. Fortunately, few people were aware of her great passion for the handsome major, and she intended to keep it that way. It was enough to know he shared her affection, even if protocol demanded that they hide it under a guise of mutual friendship.

Her thoughts were interrupted by a thunderous and discordant blast of chords from the organ. Since Priscilla was the church organist, a replacement had to be found for the occasion. An elderly woman had been brought in from North Horsham to oblige, and it was obvious that her competence on the organ was only slighter better than Priscilla's often agonizing performances.

Heads had turned toward the rear of the church in eager expectation. Wally, looking like a nervous, aging penguin in his black coattails, peeked over his shoulder for the first sight of his bride. His brother, whom Elizabeth had yet to meet, stood at his side. Neville Carbunkle was a fatter, shorter version of Wally, and he lacked the abundance of winter-white hair and beard sported by the retired sea captain.

Elizabeth was intrigued to notice that Neville seemed to be paying more attention than was appropriate to the gray-haired woman at the organ. Wally was fast approaching sixty and had mentioned that his brother was older by two years. Obviously the elder of the Carbunkle brothers was not going to be outdone by the romantic achievements of his younger sibling.

Turning her head, Elizabeth watched the procession move slowly down the long aisle, headed by an elegant middle-aged woman dressed in dark blue satin.

Earl leaned closer and whispered in her ear. "Is that Priscilla's sister?"

"Yes," Elizabeth whispered back. "That's Daphne Winterhalter."

"Doesn't look at all like Priscilla."

"Daphne's quite a bit younger. Not yet forty, I believe."

"And a heck of a lot more glamorous."

Elizabeth inclined her head. "That's her husband, Rodney. The tall, gray-haired man in the first row. He's a well-known surgeon in Cambridge. Her daughter, Tess, is one of the bridesmaids. Priscilla's friend, Fiona Farnsworth, is the other one."

Watching the bridesmaids follow sedately behind the maid of honor, Elizabeth had to admire Florrie's handiwork. The satin gowns were the same color as that worn by the maid of honor, but with shorter skirts and more daring necklines.

Priscilla's niece, Tess, looked magnificent. Shorter than her mother by several inches, she had nevertheless inherited Daphne's high cheekbones and dark, expressive eyes. Unlike Daphne's tinted auburn hair, however, the young bridesmaid's soft curls gleamed as black as a moonless sky. The slender woman at her side was closer to Priscilla's age, mid forties, but striving to look younger judging by the heavily painted lips and eyes. Her shining mane of red hair was far too startling to be natural.

"You'll meet them all later," Elizabeth whispered to Earl, as the procession halted in front of the vicar. "The Winterhalters are staying at the manor. Priscilla has only one bedroom in her flat, and she's sharing that with Fiona. They haven't seen each other for about thirty years, but —" She broke off as the organist crashed out the chords to the "Wedding March," and all heads turned again to the rear of the church.

Priscilla's white silk dress clung to her gaunt figure, making her look even more frail than usual. Her face was pale beneath the veil, and the bouquet of pink carnations and yellow freesia shook in her hand, but her smile blazed at Wally in glorious excitement and seemed to bathe the ancient walls in its glow.

She clung to the arm of a stocky, bald-headed man with a bumpy nose, who seemed uncomfortable with his appointed task. His black suit was too large for him — the sleeves of the jacket swallowed up his free hand. His bow tie hung at a dismal angle as if wishing it were anywhere but at his throat.

"Charlie Gibbons," Elizabeth murmured, in answer to Earl's raised eyebrows. "He's an old friend of Wally's. I believe they were at sea together years ago. Priscilla's parents are dead, so she asked him to give her away. He's staying with Neville in the empty cottage next door to Wally."

Earl's expression would have been comical if it hadn't been prompted by the fact that Number One, Sandhill Lane, bore a sinister reputation for being the site of two

13

murders, as well as a very close call for Elizabeth herself. She'd been unable to rent it out for that very reason.

"It was Wally's idea," she said, with a defensive shrug. "It was either there or the Tudor Arms, and Wally didn't like the idea of them staying at the pub."

The discordant thundering of the organ mercifully ceased as the bride reached Wally's side. The service was brief and quite charming, causing Elizabeth to blink back tears as the happy couple joined hands as man and wife. They appeared to float down the aisle together, and Priscilla managed to look quite radiant, while Wally beamed brighter than a lighthouse.

His smile persisted throughout the arduous process of posing for the photographs. Indeed, there were smirks on many of the faces as the fussy photographer minced around on his toes and constantly waved a languid hand at the restless group of people lined up in his lens. He wore a rather outlandish outfit of black-and-white checkered trousers, a pale blue velvet jacket, and a long, black silk scarf, drawing some irreverent comments from the male guests.

He took so long posing everyone that Elizabeth felt quite chilly standing about in

14

her flimsy frock, in spite of the balmy May afternoon. At long last the tiresome man seemed satisfied, and with Earl at her side, Elizabeth followed the crowd wandering down to the village hall.

Wally's grin continued to stretch from ear to ear during the rather rowdy reception that followed. The organist played the piano with even more gusto than she had attacked the church organ. Accompanied by the members of Priscilla's musical group, which included Wilf White on the mouth organ and a trumpeter who had earned the well-deserved stage name of Awful Ernie, the music was lively if somewhat less than harmonious.

The guests didn't seem to mind, even when Wally's brother, Neville, leapt to the stage and bellowed out a bawdy version of 'Run, Rabbit, Run.' In fact, everyone took to the dance floor and cavorted around like spring lambs. Everyone except Rita Crumm, who stood in the corner with her nose pointed at the ceiling and a look on her face that suggested she'd just swallowed a mouthful of sour milk.

The rest of her faithful followers, the devoted and often misled members of the Housewives League, having dispensed with their duties of laying out the delightfully diverse banquet, kicked up their heels with reckless abandon.

Marge Gunther, who had obviously consumed more than her share of scrumpy, got so carried away she displayed a scandalous expanse of chubby leg, giving everyone a glimpse of her corset suspenders. The sight was apparently too enticing to ignore for Neville, who leapt from the stage to join her.

Earl quietly chuckled at Elizabeth's side as he watched the antics of the revelers. "That scrumpy sure packs a punch. I can't believe plain old apple cider could have twice the alcohol of American beer. No wonder our boys get plastered when they drink it."

Elizabeth smiled. "Alfie tells me that some of them don't realize it's intoxicating until too late. He warns them all now. Apparently our cider is quite different from the cider you serve in America."

"Just as well, or we'd have kids reeling all over the school yard."

"In the fourteenth century, English children were baptized with cider. It was considered cleaner than water."

Earl looked surprised. "It's been around that long?"

"Much longer. Since before the Norman

Conquest I believe. The English climate isn't suitable for grapes, so cider became more popular than wine. Captain Cook carried it on his ship to prevent scurvy, and I understand that in the last century it was widely proclaimed as a cure for gout."

Earl lifted his beer. "Maybe I'm drinking the wrong poison."

"I'd stay with the beer if I were you. It's more predictable." Elizabeth frowned. "I wonder who that gentleman is over there." She pointed to a tall, blond man who looked to be in his late thirties. "I don't recognize him."

"Beats me." Earl took a gulp of his beer. "Probably a friend of the happy couple."

"I don't think so." She watched the man thread his way through the crowd and pause in front of Tess. "As far as I know, other than the villagers, Wally invited only two men — his brother Neville and Charlie Gibbons. Priscilla invited her sister Daphne and family, and Fiona, who brought along a gentleman friend. Priscilla did tell me his name." She wrinkled her brow. "Malcolm Ludwick, that was it."

"So maybe that guy is Ludwick."

"No, *he's* over there, dancing with Fiona." Elizabeth nodded at the vibrant redhead, whose athletic ability was quite impressive as she writhed, spun, and leapt on her long, spindly legs in a wild jitterbug. Her partner, a tall, burly man with graying hair, seemed awkward and uncomfortable as he tried to keep up with her excessive energy.

"Wow," Earl murmured. "Not bad for an old broad."

Elizabeth decided to ignore the impertinent remark. "I saw the wedding list. Priscilla asked me if I thought she'd left anyone off it who should have been invited. I'm quite sure there was no one else on it with whom I'm not familiar."

"Could have been a last-minute decision."

"I suppose so." She watched the man lay a hand on Tess's shoulder. The young girl smiled up at him and went into his arms. Elizabeth watched them dance out of sight, then forgot about them when Earl nudged her with his elbow.

"Isn't that Violet dancing with Wally's friend?"

Elizabeth stared in amazement at her sprightly housekeeper, who seemed to have shed several of her sixty-odd years as she pranced around the floor in the arms of Charlie Gibbons. "Great heavens! So it is!"

Earl grinned. "There's life in the old girl yet. I'd never have believed it."

"I wonder what Martin thinks about that." Elizabeth scanned the room to look for her butler. She'd assumed that Violet was keeping an eye on the old gentleman. Martin was well into his eighties and was not always accountable for his actions.

Having been a faithful servant to the Earl of Wellsborough's household since before the turn of the century, his failing capabilities made him more of a handicap than help at times.

Elizabeth, however, considered him part of the family, as she did Violet, the only two servants to remain with her after the misfortunes of her ex-husband had eliminated her inheritance, leaving her with a decaying old mansion and a pile of insurmountable debts.

It was thanks to the loyalty of Martin and Violet, as well as her assistant Polly and housemaid Sadie, that her lamentable situation was not common knowledge in the village. Even Earl was not aware of the extent of her predicament, though she suspected he'd guessed as much and understood that pride prevented her from discussing such mundane and depressing matters with him.

Indeed, had it not been for Earl Monroe these past months, the dreary existence of wartime England, magnified by the lack of revenue, would have been far harder to bear.

"I don't think you need worry about Martin," Earl said, breaking into her thoughts. "He's filling a large plate for himself at the table."

"Oh, heavens." Elizabeth rose to her feet. "If I don't stop him he's likely to cut himself a generous slice of the wedding cake."

"Hurry back." Earl's smile dazzled her for a moment. "I'm waiting for a slow number so I can ask you to dance."

The thought of being held in his arms made her feel quite faint. Certain that her cheeks were burning, she said hurriedly, "I'm not sure that's a good idea."

"You danced with me here once before," he reminded her.

"Ah, yes, indeed I did." She lifted her hand to make sure her hat was straight. "And if I remember, it ended in an ugly brawl from which I had to be rescued."

His grin widened. "That's what you get for trying to mix Yanks and Limeys together on the same dance floor."

She sighed. "I have to admit, it wasn't one of my better ideas."

"Well, since I'm the only 'bloody Yank' here, as the villagers are fond of calling us, you don't have to worry about anything upsetting this little shindig."

"Not unless Martin decides to sample the cake. I'd better get over there."

She left his side with reluctance. Her moments with Earl were all too brief lately. His duties at the base kept him busy, and what little time he could spare with her gave them scant opportunities for meaningful conversation. Which perhaps was just as well.

With a divorce pending, Earl had promised to keep his distance until the matter was settled. Even then, so many problems regarding their relationship would still exist. His home in America and her duty to the villagers of Sitting Marsh being the most prominent.

Elizabeth heaved a heavy sigh as she approached the rounded, frail shoulders of her butler. There were times when she heartily wished her kitchen maid mother had chosen to marry someone of her own station, instead of an earl and lord of the manor.

Martin's hand wavered under the weight of the food he'd piled on his plate. Fat, savory sausage rolls sat on top of delicate, crustless shrimp paste and cress sandwiches. Pickled onions neatly lined the plate's rim, while a slice of cold pork pie balanced on top of a wedge of Gorgonzola cheese.

"Oh, there you are, madam." Martin looked guiltily at the loaded plate. "I thought I'd have a little refreshment while Violet makes a ghastly spectacle of herself associating with that charlatan. I was told to help myself."

Elizabeth eyed the mound of food. "So I see."

Martin wavered, then said bravely, "May I offer you a morsel or two?"

"Thank you, Martin, but I think I'll wait a while." She glanced at the wedding cake, magnificent on its silver stand, and let out her breath in relief to find it untouched.

As if reading her mind, Martin murmured, "I suppose we will have to wait for the bride and groom to cut the cake."

"That is customary, Martin."

"Yes, madam. I hope the ladies remembered to bring a knife. I can't see one on the table."

"I would imagine they are waiting until they are ready to cut the cake."

As if in answer to her comment, a slight commotion turned her head. Wally was leading his bride toward the table, while behind him an urgent discussion appeared to be going on in the open doorway that led to the kitchen.

Marge Gunther, an overly plump woman with frizzy hair, stood waving her hands in agitation, while Rita Crumm, hands on hips, towered over her with a ferocious glare. Florrie Evans, the most nervous member of the group, seemed to be trying to soothe ruffled feathers without much success.

Martin mumbled something about getting a drink, but Elizabeth paid no attention to him. Obviously all was not well in the kitchen. Fortunately, the newly wedded couple seemed unaware of the commotion. Too wrapped up in each other to pay attention, no doubt.

Determined to prevent anything from spoiling this big day, Elizabeth headed purposefully toward the militant group of women. They had now been joined by Joan Plumstone, a sour-faced woman whose seemingly sole purpose in life was to cast gloom and despair everywhere she went, and Nellie Smith, the youngest and sole unmarried member of the Housewives League, who's amorous adventures were outwardly scorned and secretly envied by her peers.

As Elizabeth approached, she heard Rita

Crumm's strident tones above the clamor of music from the inept band.

"How can it be bloody missing, you twit? I saw it myself not half an hour ago."

"I don't know." Marge's whine was no less audible and Elizabeth put on a spurt.

"What on earth is going on here?" she demanded, in the most commanding voice she could muster.

Florrie uttered a little shriek and slapped a hand over her mouth.

Rita gave the startled woman a scathing glance, then turned to Elizabeth. "There is no need to concern yourself, your ladyship," she announced haughtily. "I have every-thing quite under control."

Nellie's laugh was blatantly derisive.

Rita quelled her with one of her vicious scowls.

"I would like to know what is causing this dispute," Elizabeth persisted. She glanced back at the table, where the bridal couple was now poised in front of the cake, looking somewhat confused. "As you can see, Wally and Priscilla are about to cut the cake."

Joan moaned, while Florrie muttered nervously, "Oh, dear me."

"That's the point, your ladyship," Nellie said, with a defiant look at Rita's enraged face. "The knife is missing, isn't it."

Elizabeth stared at her in confusion. "You mean the knife to cut the cake?"

Nellie nodded, while Joan moaned again.

"Well, then, get another knife. There must be others in the kitchen."

"Lady Elizabeth, you don't understand." Rita stepped forward, her face a stony mask of annoyance. "This is a very special knife. Solid silver, mother-of-pearl handle, embedded with three diamonds. It was handed down by generations of my family, for the sole purpose of slicing a wedding cake. I agreed to lend it to Priscilla for the occasion. Apart from its value, it's the only knife we have with a blade long enough to do the job properly."

"Bessie's got a bread knife in there," Nellie said helpfully. "I used it to slice the pork pie."

Rita rolled her eyes, making her scrawny features look all the more ridiculous beneath the brim of her black and white straw hat. "You can't cut a wedding cake with a bloody bread knife!" she howled.

"Yes, you can!" Elizabeth said fiercely. "Nellie, please go to the kitchen and get the knife. Make sure its clean and take it immediately to Wally. The rest of you please refrain from creating any more fuss.

This is a wedding, and we are here to help the happy couple celebrate. They are not going to care, or even notice, what they use to cut the cake. I promise you."

Looking extremely put out, Rita gathered her entourage and herded them off to the chairs that circled the dance floor. Nellie darted off and, much to Elizabeth's relief, reappeared with the bread knife. Having settled the matter to her satisfaction, Elizabeth made her way back to Earl just in time to toast the blissful couple with a glass of scrumpy.

The speeches went well, though Earl seemed to find them amusing. Elizabeth wasn't quite sure why, and she promised herself she'd ask him later. Small slices of the dark rich fruitcake topped with brittle royal icing were handed out, then came the flurry of good-byes and good wishes as the newly married pair prepared to depart on their honeymoon in the Scottish Highlands.

Florrie and Marge rushed around filling everyone's hands with what appeared to be hastily torn-up pieces of colored crepe paper. Somewhat surprised that someone hadn't thought to bring genuine confetti, Elizabeth joined everyone in throwing the tattered paper over the bride and groom as they dashed for the car that was to take them to the train station.

At last the long day was over, and satisfied that the villagers had done their best considering the limitations, Elizabeth leaned back in her chair next to Earl's and uttered a long sigh.

Earl surreptitiously squeezed her arm then withdrew his hand. "It was a swell wedding. Wally and Priscilla couldn't have asked for anything better."

Elizabeth gave him a tired smile. "It did go rather well, in spite of the upset over the missing knife." She frowned. "I must ask Rita if anyone found it. It means a great deal to her. I should hate to think someone stole it."

"Well, at least the bride and groom didn't know anything about it. They were too wrapped up in each other. Lucky stiffs."

Elizabeth smiled. "They were rather precious, weren't they. But then that's the way it should be for two people in love."

"Amen to that," Earl said softly.

The gleam in his eyes unsettled her and she looked away, pretending to scan the room. Most of the guests had left, including all three Winterhalters, Daphne, Rodney, and Tess. Polly and Sadie were nowhere to be seen, and had most likely joined some of the other guests who had earlier announced their intention of continuing the celebrations at the Tudor Arms.

The band, whose members seemed determined to outlast everyone in the room, reached a crashing finale to the song they were playing. A smattering of applause echoed hollowly in the near empty hall. Elizabeth was about to suggest it was time to leave when an ear-splitting shriek rebounded among the rafters of the high ceiling.

"What the heck was that?" Earl stared in the direction of the kitchen, from where the scream had erupted.

Elizabeth was already on her feet and heading for the source of the commotion. The door flew open as she reached it and Florrie stumbled out into the hall, her hand over her mouth. "Ooh," she moaned, "I'm going to be sick."

Nellie appeared in the doorway and stared wide-eyed at Elizabeth.

"What's happened?" Elizabeth demanded, prepared for the worst.

She felt a chill when Nellie said in an odd, matter-of-fact voice, "They found the wedding cake knife, your ladyship."

Something told her she wasn't going to like the answer, but she asked anyway. "Where was it?"

"It's in the basement." Nellie's voice rose to an unnatural high pitch. "It's sticking out the chest of a dead bloke."

Chapter 2

"I'll call the constables," Earl said, as Elizabeth headed across the kitchen between the yellow vinyl-covered tables to the cellar door.

"Oh, would you?" Elizabeth waved her thanks. "There's a telephone box across the street. Or ask the vicar if you may use his telephone. I think he's gone home."

Close to the cellar, Bessie leaned against the wall, her face chalk white. Oh, don't go down there, m'm," she mumbled, when Elizabeth reached her. "It's such an 'orrible sight, it is."

"I just want to take a look." Elizabeth sent a glance of apprehension at the steps leading to the cellar. "Who is it? Did you recognize him?"

"One of the wedding guests, m'm. I don't know his name." Bessie mopped her brow with her apron. "I don't know what's been going on here, 'onest, I don't. I thought it strange when we couldn't find the key to the door. Locked it were, and I know it weren't locked when we got here. I put the confetti down there so's no one would get to it before Wally and Priscilla left but then when I went to get it the door was locked and we couldn't find the key and we were all so upset about not being able to get the confetti but Mrs. Crumm had the brilliant idea to tear up some of the decorations into pieces to make it look like confetti and we all got busy on that and I never gave the key another thought until Florrie found it just now in the jug of milk and . . ."

She paused for breath, giving Elizabeth a chance to ask, "You found the key where?"

"In a jug of milk, m'm. Well, actually, the jug were empty. Florrie was going to wash it out and she heard something rattling and there was the key. Of course, by then it was too late, wasn't it. Wally and Priscilla had already gone. I should have known then that something was going on."

"So you were the one to find the body?"

Bessie swept a stray lock of gray hair back from her eyes. "Yes, m'm. I went down there to get the confetti, you see, so's I could take it back to the shop and get me money back, seeing as how we didn't use it an' all. That's when I saw — ." She gulped, and tears filled her eyes. "It was so awful, m'm. There he was, just lying there with Mrs. Crumm's fancy knife sticking out his

31

chest and all covered in blood, it were. I wouldn't let no one else go down there."

Elizabeth patted the woman's shoulder. "There, there, Bessie. Pull yourself together. Why don't you get yourself a nice cup of tea or perhaps some of that delicious scrumpy. I'm sure you'll feel better in no time."

"Thank you, m'm. I think I will."

To Elizabeth's relief, Bessie hurried off and disappeared behind the little knot of women gathered in the doorway. Rita, as usual, was ordering everyone to be calm, while sounding somewhat hysterical herself.

"Perhaps it would be better if everyone would wait in the main hall," Elizabeth called out. "The constable will be here soon and he'll take care of everything. Meanwhile you can get on with the cleaning up. I'm sure you all want to get home as soon as possible."

Obviously annoyed at having matters taken out of her hands, Rita sent her a haughty look, but nevertheless shepherded her flock out of the kitchen, just as Earl squeezed past them to come back in.

"I'm so glad to see you," Elizabeth said, as he strode toward her. "I really wasn't looking forward to going down there by myself."

"Why do you need to go down there at all?" he demanded when he reached her. "The P.C. will be here any minute." She made a face at him and he shrugged. "Right. Stupid question. OK, let's go. But I'm going first."

Nervous about what might be waiting for her down there, she was only too happy to follow him down the stairs.

The body lay crumpled at the bottom of the steps. Trying not to notice the knife sticking out from the blood soaked jacket, Elizabeth said unsteadily, "It's the man we saw earlier. Remember? I pointed him out. I was wondering who he was."

Earl grunted. "Well, at least it's not anyone you know. That's got to be a relief."

"Yes, I suppose it is." Elizabeth frowned, then crouched down to touch the floor with her fingers. "Confetti," she murmured, as she stared at the tiny pieces of colored paper. "Bessie must have dropped it when she saw the body —" She broke off as a gruff voice spoke from the head of the steps.

" 'Ere, 'ere! Wot's going on down there, then?"

Elizabeth shaded her eyes against the harsh light of the bare lightbulb. "Oh, there you are, George. I'm afraid we've

33

had a bit of bother down here. You had better come and take a look."

George ducked his head so that his helmet cleared the door frame. "Is that you, your ladyship? Not interfering with the evidence, I trust?"

"Of course not, George. You know better than that."

"Who's that with you, then?" George demanded as he clumped down the steps.

"It's me, Constable." Earl lifted his hand in a salute.

"Ho, yes, Major Monroe," George muttered, managing to make the name sound like a contagious disease. "Might have known it were you."

Elizabeth decided to ignore the subtle disapproval behind the words. "The major and I were trying to identify the victim. I don't suppose you know who he is, George?"

The constable reached the bottom of the steps, peered at the victim, shoved his helmet further back on his head with his thumb, and frowned. "Looks like he's been stabbed," he remarked.

"Amazing deduction," Earl murmured.

Elizabeth dug him in the ribs with her elbow and was rewarded by a faint, "Oof!"

Luckily George was squatting next to the

victim and seemed not to hear the comment. "Can't say as I know this bloke," he muttered. "Was he one of the wedding guests?"

"Well, that's rather a difficult question to answer," Elizabeth said, as George started going through the dead man's pockets. "We saw him on the dance floor, but I don't remember him being included on the guest list. The major suggested he might have been added at the last minute. Perhaps some of the other guests might know who he is."

"Not many of them left up there now." Apparently having found nothing useful, George got up with a grunt. "Should have had them all stay put, your ladyship. It's going to make things difficult with the questioning now."

"Yes, well, I would have, George, if I'd known there was going to be a murder taking place."

George narrowed his eyes, peering at her in the gloom. "Perhaps you and the major should join the others, m'm. I'll have to send for the doctor, and the inspector will want to know about this, too."

"I can't imagine why," Elizabeth muttered to no one in particular as she climbed the steps. "He seldom bothers to pay any attention to our little mishaps."

"I'd say this is a bit more than a little mishap," Earl said, following her into the kitchen.

"You're right, of course. What an unfortunate end to such a lovely day. Now there will be an investigation and everyone will be upset. Thank goodness Wally and Priscilla left before the poor devil was discovered. At least they don't have to know about this until after the honeymoon. I should hate for anything to spoil that for them."

George's heavy footsteps sounded behind her. "I'd like to question the guests now, your ladyship," he announced.

"Very well." With a heavy sigh, Elizabeth led him into the main hall, where a small forlorn group of guests huddled in one corner.

Rita, of course, was the first to speak up. "I hope you're not going to keep us hanging around all evening, George. Some of us have homes to go to, you know."

George gave her a baleful glare. "I won't keep anyone longer than I have to. Now, first, I need the name of the unfortunate victim."

"I don't see how we can tell you that," Rita retorted, "seeing as how we don't know who's been killed."

"It's the tall gentleman," Elizabeth said helpfully. "He has blond hair and is wearing a dark gray suit with a blue silk tie."

"Oo, I remember 'im," Nellie Smith piped up. "Handsome bugger, he was. Who would want to kill a nice-looking bloke like that? What a bloomin' waste."

Rita turned on her at once. "Is that all you can think about? How handsome he was? He's lying down there with a knife in his chest. Have you no respect for the dead, Nellie Smith?"

"Of course I do," Nellie said hotly. "I only meant —"

"And how did you know he had a knife in his chest?" George demanded.

Rita tossed her head. "It happens to be my knife, doesn't it. Bessie told me where it was." Her voice lost some of its bravado when she added, "I'll never use that knife again to cut another wedding cake. Not after knowing where it's been."

"I just can't believe he's dead," Bessie said, her voice still quivering. "I was just talking to him in the kitchen an hour or so ago. What a dreadful thing to happen. Thank the Lord Wally and Priscilla got away before I found the body."

George looked around. "Seems as if a lot

37

of people got away," he said darkly. "What I want to know is, what's the name of the deceased? Someone's got to know who he is."

Neville Carbunkle, who had been hovering around in the background, stepped forward. "Well, I can tell you one thing," he said. "Wally didn't know him. I heard him asking someone who he was."

George pulled a notepad from his top pocket, then spent an agonizing minute or two hunting for a pencil. Having found one in his trousers pocket, he licked the end of it and started scribbling.

"The chap he asked didn't know the bloke, either," Neville added, "but I did see the . . . er . . . deceased having nasty words with the photographer earlier."

Bessie smothered a gasp with her hand.

George turned to her. "Got something to say, Bessie?"

Bessie fanned her face with her hand. "Well, it's just . . . when I spoke to the dead man . . . well, he wasn't dead when I spoke to him, of course, but you know what I mean . . ."

George loudly cleared his throat. "Just refer to the deceased as the deceased, then we'll all know what you mean."

Bessie nodded, gulped, then said in a

rush, "Well, the deceased, who wasn't deceased yet, asked me for some confetti and I said, What for? 'cause I wasn't ready to bring it up yet and I told him I was going to bring it up right before the wedding couple left and he said he wanted it to play a joke on Dickie, so I said what sort of joke and he said it was just a bit of fun and I said as how Dickie didn't like jokes very much and he said he'd like this one and I said —"

"Hold on, hold on," George butted in, sounding irritable. "I can't write all that down when you're rattling on so fast, can I."

Bessie drew a breath. "I just wanted to tell you —"

"Wait a minute." George looked over his notes, mumbling, "Wanted to play a joke." He looked up again. "Who's Dickie?"

"The photographer," Bessie explained. "Dickie Muggins. He lives in North Horsham and his mother comes into my tea shop all the time. I told Priscilla about him and she asked him to take the photographs for the wedding."

"Bit of a nance that one, if you ask me," Neville muttered.

George ignored him. "So what was this joke all about, then?"

Bessie frowned. "Well, he wouldn't tell

me, would he. I told him the confetti was in the cellar and it were staying there until I was ready to bring it up."

George went on writing. "Is this Dickie Muggins still here?" he asked, when he lifted his head again.

"No," Elizabeth told him. "I saw him leave right after Wally and Priscilla left."

George nodded. "Thank you, m'm." He looked at Neville. "You said you heard Mr. Muggins arguing with the deceased?"

"I didn't hear them. I saw them." Neville gestured toward the kitchen. "I was dancing by the door and I saw the photographer shake his fist in the victim's face and I could tell he was worked up about something."

"When was this, then?"

"It was before they cut the cake and made all those speeches. I know that, because I was dancing with Marge at the time."

Everyone looked at Marge, who blushed and giggled like a young girl.

The sight reminded Elizabeth of the way Violet looked in Charlie Gibbons's arms. Elizabeth looked around for her, but she was nowhere to be seen. "Has anyone seen Violet and Martin?" she asked, interrupting whatever George was saying.

He frowned in disapproval but waited for someone to answer her.

"I think they went home with the Winterhalters," Nellie offered. "They were riding in that big black motorcar."

"Lucky buggers," Marge Gunther muttered. "We all have to walk home."

"Well, it's not as far as the Manor House, is it," Nellie said.

George loudly cleared his throat. "If I may have your attention, would someone please tell me who invited the deceased to the wedding and what his name is?"

"Well I should think," Elizabeth said mildly, "that if Wally didn't know him, he couldn't have invited him, so he must be a friend of Priscilla's."

"No," a voice declared from the back of the group. "Prissy didn't invite him either." Priscilla's flamboyant schoolfriend pushed to the front of the group. "She never set eyes on him until today."

George gazed up at Fiona with obvious admiration for a full second, then coughed and looked down at his notepad. "And you are?"

"Mrs. Fiona Farnsworth. I'm an old friend of the bride."

George scribbled again. "Well now, if Captain Carbunkle didn't invite the deceased, and Miss Pierce — or I should say Mrs. Carbunkle now — didn't invite him, then who in blue blazes did invite him?"

"Maybe you should ask the other brides-maid." Fiona's companion had stepped up behind her. "I understand they knew each other very well."

Fiona stared at her escort. "Tess? How'd you know that?"

Malcolm's smile was indulgent as he laid an arm across Fiona's shoulders. "I heard them talking, my love. Actually, *arguing* would be a better word. The young lady was furious with him."

His last remark had been directed at George, who was furiously scribbling on his notepad. "And you are?"

"Malcolm Ludwig, old chap. I'm engaged to be married to this lovely lady here."

"Well, that's two people already who didn't like the bloke," George muttered. "I'll need to have the photographer's address and phone number, and I'll have a word with that young lady. What's her name?"

"Tess Winterhalter," Elizabeth answered him. "I understand she went down to the Tudor Arms with some of the other guests. I'm sure she'll be back soon. If you like,

42

you can come up to the manor later and talk to her. Her parents will be there, as well."

Her concern was for the young girl, who would no doubt feel more secure in being questioned by the police if her parents were present.

George, however, murmured, "Good idea, your ladyship. I should like to question the young lady's parents, anyhow, seeing as how the deceased was a friend of their daughter."

"Does that mean we can all go home now?" Rita demanded peevishly.

"Not so fast," George declared, as the ladies made a general movement to disperse. "I want to know if anyone saw anything unusual."

"We saw Marge's knickers," Nellie said, with a wicked leer.

Marge gasped above the titters from the group. "You did not!"

George loudly cleared his throat. "I meant anything that might help in this 'orrible murder investigation."

The faces sobered as silence fell over the crowd.

"I'm sure if anyone remembers anything he or she will let you know," Elizabeth said. Addressing everyone in general, she added more loudly, "I'm sure we all want to find out who committed this terrible deed, do we not?"

A feeble chorus of agreement answered her and she turned back to George. "I'm leaving for the manor now, George. I assume you will wait for Dr. Sheridan. Shall we expect you later?"

"Thank you, m'm. Much obliged, I'm sure." George touched the narrow brim of his helmet and tucked the notepad in his pocket. "In the meantime, I must ask everyone who attended the wedding and doesn't live here to stay in Sitting Marsh until I've had a chance to question them."

There were mutters of protest from some of the guests, and everyone started talking amongst themselves.

Feeling somewhat unsettled herself, Elizabeth led the way from the hall, followed by Earl, with George close behind. Furtive glances from some of the women were directed at them as they left. Well aware that speculation was rife in the village about her relationship with the major, Elizabeth was constantly on guard against fueling the gossip.

There were times, however, when she refused to sacrifice what little time she could scrounge with him, which is why she'd accepted his offer to drive her to the church in his Jeep. No matter what the villagers might make of that. In any case, riding with Earl was a little more elegant than sitting astride her motorcycle, which was her usual mode of transport.

Roaring up the hill in the Jeep toward the manor, she contemplated the disturbing events. If the stranger was indeed a friend of Tess's and had been invited to the wedding by her, the poor child was in for a terrible shock when she heard the news.

Which brought up the question: if he was a friend of hers, why would she go to the Tudor Arms without him? Had they quarreled, as Malcolm had suggested? If so, things wouldn't look too good for Tess.

"Well, at least they can't blame this one on the three musketeers."

Earl's voice, raised to be heard above the roar of the engine, startled her. "I'd almost forgotten about them," she called back. "Are you still having problems with them?"

"Three of our vehicles were disabled last weekend. Our guys had to walk back to base. I just wish I could get my hands on them. We have enough problems to deal with right now, without worrying about a bunch of hoodlums bent on mischief. If this keeps up someone's going to get hurt."

"Oh, dear." Ever since Elizabeth had heard about the three masked men from London visiting American bases and damaging property to harass the American servicemen, she'd been worried that their mischief-making would escalate into real violence.

Or even that the Americans would retaliate with disastrous results. So far the skirmishes had caused little more than a few bruises. But there was a limit to the victims' patience, especially when they were already dealing with unbelievable stress.

"I can't believe they're getting away with it," Earl said, as they tore around the curve on the hill. "They've got the military hunting for them, as well as your constables. You'd think someone would be able to grab them."

"Apparently they're extremely adept at slipping the noose." Thankful for the long twilight evenings, Elizabeth hung on grimly as the Jeep swayed from side to side. Riding at this speed was infinitely more dangerous in the dark, thanks to the blackout, which forbade lights on all vehicles and in all windows. "They've had a lot of practice."

"Yeah, you're right about that." Earl

straightened out the wheel. "So, any ideas who might have killed the wedding guest back there?"

"Hardly. We don't even know why he was at the wedding."

"Well, if the bridesmaid knew him, I guess her parents will know him, too."

"That's what I'm hoping." Elizabeth frowned. The Winterhalters had left immediately after the cake had been cut, apparently taking her butler and housekeeper with them. She sincerely hoped that Martin was not the cause of their hasty departure. He was not used to attending social events and rarely left the manor these days. Though he had seemed quite well when she'd spoken to him.

Feeling uneasy, she was relieved when Earl pulled up to the steps with a scrunch of tires. "The night is still young," she said, as he helped her climb out of the Jeep. "Would you like to join me in a glass of sherry?"

To her disappointment, he shook his head. "I've got some paperwork to catch up on, and I have to make a real early start in the morning. Rain check?"

She smiled at him. "Of course. Good night, then."

He still had hold of her hand, and he

held on to it for a moment longer before letting her go. "You'll let me know if you get involved in this mess, right?"

"Don't I always?"

"Not until you're knee deep in trouble, as a rule."

"I promise I'll keep you informed."

He lifted his hand and gently stroked her cheek. "I'm gonna hold you to that. Just watch your step, okay? Don't go charging ahead until you know what you're getting into."

She covered his fingers with her own. "You worry too much."

"Yeah, I guess I do. I just don't want anything bad to happen to you. You're my lucky charm, you know."

He'd said the words lightly, but she knew, only too well, the significance behind them. Every time he took to the skies he was in far more danger than she could ever be. The chances of him coming back grew slimmer with each mission. Like so many others who flew into dire peril each day, he was convinced that as long as he had someone there waiting for him, he would survive.

"And you are mine," she reminded him. "As long as you need me, I'll always be here for you. Just make sure you come back to me."

She saw the light in his eyes change. He stared down at her for a long moment, then dropped his hand. *"Damn,"* he muttered softly. "So long, Elizabeth. See you soon."

She nodded, her heart too full to answer. Hurrying up the steps, she resisted the urge to watch him drive away. Every time she left him, she never knew if it would be her last sight of him. If it was, she didn't want it to be the image of him leaving her.

Chapter 3

Polly gazed mournfully around the crowded, noisy pub and wondered why the heck she'd bothered to go down there. Sadie, her round cheeks flushed and her light brown hair stuck out the sides of her head like two ears of corn, was at the dartboard surrounded by a bunch of rowdy GIs. The rest of the guests from the wedding were at the piano making a horrible noise with their singing.

Polly reached for her gin and orange and took a sip. Nothing was going right lately. Nothing had gone right since Marlene had left to drive ambulances in Italy. She missed her older sister more than she ever thought she would.

She missed Sam even more. Sam Cutter, the man she thought she was going to marry, had gone back to America. Without her. She still couldn't believe it. All because he thought she was too young for him. Almost sixteen years old, she'd been then, and he thought she was too young. Well, that was the last time she'd ever look at another Yank.

With a flick of her wrist, she drained her glass. She was fed up. Even Sadie, her best mate, had deserted her tonight. She might as well go home.

She slapped the glass down on the table, but before she could push her chair back a young woman plopped down on the chair opposite her and demanded, "You're Polly, aren't you? Lady Elizabeth's assistant?"

It took Polly a moment to recognize the bridesmaid Sadie had brought down to the pub with her. Tess Winterhalter looked quite different wearing a skirt and blouse instead of the beautiful blue frock she'd worn at the wedding. Her face looked different, too. Her lipstick had worn off and her eyes looked puffy, as if she'd been crying.

"Yeah, I'm Polly Barnett."

"I'm Tess. My family came down from Cambridge for the wedding."

Polly eyed the newcomer warily. She'd been shocked when Sadie had told her she'd befriended Priscilla's niece. Everyone knew that Priscilla's sister had married above her. People with money who spoke all proper like that usually didn't mix with the poorer class. Especially a housemaid like Sadie. "Yeah, I know," she said. "Sadie told me all about you."

51

"Sadie makes me laugh," Tess said, though she didn't look like she wanted to laugh right then.

Polly gazed with envy at the bridesmaid's black curls. Her own hair was black, too, but it hung as straight as a blackout curtain. She'd give anything to have curls like that. No wonder the Yanks were looking at her. She looked like a flipping film star.

Tess seemed not to notice the flirty looks coming her way. Something had upset her, that much Polly could tell. The girl sat twisting her glass around in her hands as if it were someone's neck she were wringing. "Sadie's playing darts over there," she said, her voice low enough that Polly had to strain to hear her above the racket the dart players were making.

"She's always playing darts." Polly shot a look at the dartboard as a cheer went up from that corner. "She comes down here a lot. She likes playing 'cos she nearly always wins. She says it makes her feel good to beat the boys at something."

"There's not much else to do for excitement in this place, is there."

Polly shrugged. "Depends who you're with, I suppose."

"I know. There's someone I . . ." Tess's face crumpled, and she covered her mouth with her hand as if to smother a sob.

Polly felt a stirring of sympathy. She knew what it felt like to miss someone. "I'm sorry," she murmured awkwardly.

After a moment or two, the other girl seemed to get herself under control. "Well, my father will be happy. He hated Brian. He kept telling me he was too old for me and that he was only after me for the money." She looked up, her face clouded with misery. "Brian was only thirty-three. Daddy made him sound positively ancient."

Polly's attention sparked, in spite of herself. After all, this was a subject dear to her heart. "So how old are you then?"

"Twenty." Tess hunted in her pocket and found a handkerchief. She blew her nose with it, then crumpled it in a ball in her hands. "It's only thirteen years' difference."

Thirteen years! There'd been only seven years difference between her and Sam. Deciding she had something in common with this hoity-toity miss, after all, Polly found herself telling her all about her and Sam. "Everything was going fine," she finished, "until he had an accident in the Jeep and messed up his face. I know it was because he couldn't stand me looking at his scars."

Tess shuddered. "How awful. Where is he now?"

"Gone back to America, hasn't he." Just thinking about him made her own eyes prickle with tears. "I'll never see him again."

Tess leaned forward. "You're still young. You'll find someone else."

"I don't think so. I tried it once, but I picked the wrong bloke. He turned out to be a criminal."

Tess's eyes widened in shock. "How absolutely rotten for you!"

"It was," Polly agreed gloomily. "I don't seem to have any luck with men. Really I don't."

"Well, I'm sure you'll meet someone nice soon." Tess shook her head. "I thought Brian was going to be the man of my dreams, but I was wrong." Her face turned suddenly ugly, startling Polly. "I hate to say it, but Daddy was right about him after all."

"So what happened?" Polly asked, now glued to her chair.

"Well, we'd been seeing each other on and off for quite a while. Behind Daddy's back, of course. I told Brian I was going to be in Sitting Marsh for the wedding, so I wouldn't be able to see him this weekend.

But then I missed him so much, and I was pretty bored that first night at the manor, so when Sadie offered to bring me down here I thought it would be fun."

Polly nodded. "Sadie told me you'd come down here with her on Thursday night."

Tess sighed and passed a hand across her forehead. "Yes, well, the first thing we saw when we walked in was Brian sitting at the bar. I never dreamed he would follow me down here. He said he was staying at the pub, and that he planned to go to the wedding reception so we could be there together."

Impressed by this bold move, Polly said breathlessly, "You must have been so thrilled!"

Tess shrugged. "Not really. To tell you the truth, I wished he hadn't come. I knew Daddy would be livid, and I didn't want to spoil the wedding for Aunt Prissy. I told Brian he couldn't come to the reception. He said he hadn't come all that way to sit around the pub by himself all weekend. We had a nasty row and he stalked off. I thought he'd gone home, but then he turned up at the reception this afternoon."

Polly sucked in her breath. "So what did your dad say when he found out?"

"Well, he was livid, of course. Just as I thought. He called Brian a swindler, said he was using me and that he was only after the money. He told Brian if he came near me again he'd have him arrested for harassment."

"So did he leave?"

"No, he wanted to dance with me." Tess's lower lip trembled. "I was really angry with Daddy. I loved Brian and I told Daddy if he didn't let me see him I'd run away with him. I knew Daddy wouldn't make a scene at the wedding, so I danced with Brian anyway."

Polly frowned. "I don't remember seeing you with anyone. Which one was he?"

"The tall fellow, in the dark gray suit and blue tie."

"Oh, him." Polly nodded. "Nice-looking bloke."

"Yes, I suppose he is." Tess drummed on the table with her fingers. "It's just a shame he turned out to be such a rotter."

"So what'd he do then?" Polly demanded. But before Tess could answer, another voice broke into the conversation.

"Come on, Pol, let's go and join the singalong at the piano." Sadie's grin took in both of them. "You, too, Tess. We need some girls over there to drown out the Yanks."

Polly looked at Tess, who shook her head. "I'm tired. I think I'll go back to the Manor House. Where can I call for a taxi?"

Sadie burst out laughing. "You're joking. There's no taxi in Sitting Marsh."

Tess stared up at her in dismay. "Then how am I going to get home?"

"Well, I could give you a ride on me bicycle," Sadie said doubtfully, then shook her head. "Nah. We'd never get up the hill. Wait here." She bolted back to the crowd at the dartboard, where she grabbed the arm of an American serviceman.

"Looks like you'll be going home in a Jeep," Polly said, as Sadie gestured at them.

"Oh, help." Tess sighed. "Well, I suppose it's better than walking all that way. These shoes have such high heels I'd have blisters all over my feet by the time I got there."

Sadie came back to the table, dragging a shy-looking soldier with close-cropped red hair and worried eyes. "Here," Sadie announced, "this is Joe. He's a good friend of mine. He'll give us a lift to the Manor House."

Joe stared anxiously at Tess. "It's not a very comfortable ride, ma'am, I —"

"Oh, stop worrying, Joe!" Sadie gave his arm a little shake. "It'll be a lark. I can throw me bicycle in the back. You can give Polly a lift, too." She winked at Polly. "That's if you're ready to go home?"

"More than ready." Polly got to her feet. "I've got me bicycle with me, though."

"There won't be room for all of you as well as two bikes," Joe protested.

"It's all right." Polly picked up her handbag and shoved it under her arm. "I'd rather ride, anyway." She left before Sadie could talk her out of it. The truth was, it hurt to see Sadie so happy with her boyfriend. Polly tried not to let it bother her, but seeing them together only reminded her of when she was happy too, with Sam. She would never be happy like that again.

To Elizabeth's dismay, it was Violet who answered her summons on the bell rope. As the huge front door swung open, she bounced inside, asking breathlessly, "Is Martin all right? He's not ill, is he?"

Violet clicked her tongue. "Calm down, Lizzie. You'll give yourself a heart attack with all your worrying. Martin is in bed, sleeping off the glass of scrumpy he managed to gulp down when I wasn't looking. Went straight to his head, it did, silly old goat. I warned him not to touch it. The Winterhalters were nice enough to bring us home in their motorcar. Really posh it is. The sort of motorcar you should have, Lizzie, instead of that noisy, smelly old motorbike. Your father would turn in his grave if he saw you riding that around the village, I'm sure. Not at all what a lady should be riding, that's for certain."

Elizabeth followed her down to the kitchen, paying scant attention to her housekeeper's prattling. Settling herself at the kitchen table, she watched Violet fill the kettle with cold water. "What about the Winterhalters? Are they here? I didn't see the motorcar when I came in."

"Desmond put it in the stables for them. Can't leave a nice motorcar like that out all night. They're in the library. I took up a bottle of that good Scotch your major brought over. I thought that nice Mr. Winterhalter was going to kiss me, he was so pleased. Can't get good Scotch for love nor money nowadays, he told me."

Deciding she couldn't put it off any longer, Elizabeth said carefully, "Well, you all missed a good deal of excitement at the wedding."

Violet set the kettle on the stove and lit the gas under it. "Don't tell me. Rita Crumm drank too much scrumpy and did a striptease on the tables."

Surprised her housekeeper even knew about such things, Elizabeth almost laughed. "No," she said. "I'm afraid it's a lot more serious than that. Bessie found a dead body in the cellar."

Violet spun around, one hand over her mouth. "Go on! Who was it?"

"Well, no one seems to know. Apparently he wasn't invited to the wedding, though one of the guests thought Tess might be acquainted with him." She glanced up at the clock. "In fact, I think I'll pop upstairs and have a word with the Winterhalters before George gets here. I want to warn them. It's quite possible they might know the gentleman."

"What happened to him?" Violet asked, as Elizabeth headed for the door.

"Someone stabbed him in the chest with the missing knife that was supposed to cut the wedding cake."

"Oh, my. I imagine Rita was put out about that."

"She wasn't too pleased, to say the least." Elizabeth paused at the door. "When George arrives, see if you can keep him busy down here until I get back."

Without waiting for her housekeeper to answer, she let the door close behind her and headed for the stairs.

She found Rodney and Daphne seated in the library, each immersed in a book. They had both changed out of their wedding finery — Rodney now in a dark red velvet smoking jacket and Daphne wearing a fetching housecoat covered in pink and white embroidery.

They looked up as she entered, and Rodney immediately sprang to his feet.

"Oh, there you are, Lady Elizabeth!" he exclaimed, his voice overly loud and jovial. "Our apologies for leaving the festivities so abruptly. The little woman had a headache, didn't you, precious."

Daphne gave him a nervous smile. "Did I? Yes, of course. I did."

The infuriated look he gave her made Elizabeth uncomfortable. Obviously, the Winterhalters were having some kind of disagreement. "I'm afraid I have some bad news for you," she said, coming straight to the point. "It concerns a gentleman guest at the wedding. A rather tall chap wearing a dark gray suit and light blue silk tie. Was he a friend of yours?"

Daphne stared blankly at her, while Rodney's eyes narrowed. "If you are referring to Brian Sutcliffe, he's nothing but a two-timing fortune hunter. He barged into the wedding uninvited and made a general nuisance of himself. The man is a rake of the worst kind."

"Rodney is absolutely right," Daphne agreed fervently. "The man is a cheat and a liar. I can't imagine what my daughter sees in that charlatan."

"In that case," Elizabeth said quietly, "I imagine neither of you will be too upset to hear that someone killed him this afternoon."

Rodney Winterhalter met her gaze without so much as a blink. "Is that so."

Somewhat taken aback by his indifference, Elizabeth was lost for words.

Then, in the silence that followed, Daphne gasped, then whispered fearfully, "My God, Rodney. What have you done?"

Elizabeth watched Rodney's face as he stared at his wife, his eyes burning with fury. "What the devil are you talking about, Daphne? I didn't stick a knife in the blasted chap, if that's what you're thinking."

Daphne looked as if she didn't believe him, and Elizabeth said hastily, "I think I should warn you that police constable Dalrymple is on his way up here to question Tess. By all accounts, she was one of the last people to see the gentleman alive."

A worried expression clouded Daphne's face. "Oh, dear. I do hope —" She broke off, and stared helplessly at her husband.

"Don't be ridiculous," Rodney snapped. He turned to Elizabeth. "I'm quite sure my daughter has nothing to do with this. Unfortunately she was quite infatuated with the rotter."

"I don't —" Daphne was interrupted by the sound of a sharp tap on the door.

At Elizabeth's command to enter, the door opened and Sadie poked her head into the space. "Pardon me, your ladyship," she said, flicking a glance at the Winterhalters, "but Violet said to tell you P.C. Dalrymple is in the kitchen."

"Thank you, Sadie."

The girl nodded and started to withdraw her head when Rodney asked sharply, "Did Tess come home with you?"

Sadie opened the door wider. "Yes, sir. My friend gave her a ride home in his Jeep a while ago."

Daphne rolled her eyes in horror, but Rodney merely nodded. "Be so kind as to tell her I wish to speak to her. Now."

"Yes, sir, but I think she's gone to bed."

"Then get her out of bed," Rodney ordered harshly. "I want to speak to her before the constable gets to her."

Sadie's eyebrows rose and her eyes widened as she looked at Elizabeth.

"It's all right, Sadie," Elizabeth said quietly. "Do as Mr. Winterhalter asks at once."

"Yes, m'm." Sadie's face disappeared and the door closed with a quiet snap.

Daphne folded her arms across her chest and started rocking back and forth, while Rodney paced across the soft carpet to the bookshelves and back again.

"You don't mind if I stay?" Elizabeth murmured, as she took a seat across from Daphne.

Daphne shook her head, while Rodney muttered, "Of course not, your ladyship. We have nothing to hide."

Elizabeth attempted to make light conversation, but her efforts were largely ignored, and she was quite relieved when the door opened and Tess, wearing a yellow silk robe tied with a black silk sash, wandered into the room.

"You got me out of bed," she said, as her parents turned to face her. "Couldn't it wait until tomorrow?"

"We have something to tell you," Rodney began, but Daphne sprang to her feet.

"Let me tell her," she said, the words more a command than a request.

Rodney turned away with an impatient

flick of his head. "Very well. But be quick about it. That police chap will be here any second."

Tess sent a startled look his way. "Police?"

"Tess . . ." Daphne approached her daughter and seized both her hands. "You must be brave, darling. It's about Brian."

Tess's face froze. "Brian? What about him?"

"I'm afraid —" Daphne's voice broke and she dipped her head.

Rodney grunted in exasperation, then said bluntly, "He's dead."

Daphne's cry of protest was drowned out by Tess's shocked howl. "No! I don't believe you. He can't be dead. I just saw him this afternoon. How can he be dead?"

"Someone stabbed him with a knife." Rodney strode over to the young girl, who had begun to sob, and pushed his wife aside. Grasping Tess's shoulders, he said more quietly, "I know this must be a shock to you, child, but you must pull yourself together. The constable wants to have a word with you, and you need your wits about you."

"I don't want to talk to anyone," Tess sobbed. "I just want to go home."

"I'm sure —" Elizabeth began, but once

more she was interrupted by a tap on the door.

This time it was Violet who stood in the doorway. "I'm sorry, madam, but the constable insisted on coming right up."

Elizabeth nodded at her housekeeper. "It's all right, Violet. You may show the constable in."

"Yes, madam." Violet opened the door to allow the portly figure of George to pass through, then closed it behind him.

"Good evening, your ladyship," George said, removing his helmet and tucking it under his arm.

Elizabeth got her feet and made the introductions. None of the Winterhalters were particularly gracious. Dahpne seemed bewildered, frightened, and out of her depth. Rodney's face was carved in stone, while Tess continued to hiccup softly as sobs escaped her lips.

"Now, then, young lady," George said, after licking the end of his pencil, "when was the last time you saw the deceased?"

Tears rolled down Tess's face as she struggled to answer him. "This afternoon."

"I understand," George said pompously, "that you were arguing with the deceased shortly before his death."

Tess cried louder and hunted in her

pocket for a handkerchief. Daphne pulled one from her sleeve and handed it to her. "Here you are, darling. Just tell the policeman what he wants to know."

"I told him I never wanted to see him again!" Tess howled. "I didn't mean it!"

George scribbled on his notepad. "I see. And what prompted you to say that to him, might I ask?"

Tess appeared to make a valiant effort to control her weeping. "I found out he . . . he was with another woman at the Tudor Arms. She was in his *room*." The last word rose on a wail of anguish.

"Always knew the miserable cad was no good," Rodney muttered.

"Why didn't you tell us, darling?" Daphne cried, obviously distressed.

"I didn't want anyone else to know what a fool I'd been," Tess managed, between sobs.

George went on scribbling some more. "So what happened when you told him you didn't want to see him no more?"

"He was angry. I . . . ran away."

"And he was alive when you left him?"

"I . . . I just wanted to get away from him."

"Of course you did, dear," Daphne said. She threw a protective arm about her daughter's shoulders. "You can see the child has had a terrible shock," she said, glaring at George. "Can't this wait until to-morrow?"

"Just a couple more questions, madam, if you don't mind." George turned to Rodney. "When did you last see the de-ceased alive?"

"At the reception. I told him to leave. He was hanging around my daughter and making a blasted nuisance of himself."

"I take it you had no liking for the de-ceased."

Rodney uttered a bark of contempt. "I had no time for the rotter, no. He was ha-rassing my daughter."

"And you wanted to stop him doing that," George said, busily writing.

Rodney's face grew redder. "Yes, I did. That doesn't mean I killed him."

"No, sir, but it does mean you had a reason to want him out of the way, so to speak." George lifted his head. "As did the young lady, apparently." He snapped his notebook shut with an air of authority. "I must ask you all to stay in Sitting Marsh until the inspector can have a word with you. I'm putting you under house arrest on suspicion of being involved in a murder."

Chapter 4

For a moment everyone was shocked into silence, then Tess wailed a protest, echoed by an exclamation from Daphne.

"George —" Elizabeth began, but the constable lifted his hand.

"Begging your pardon, your ladyship, but I must ask you to refrain from interfering in police business."

Rodney uttered a snort of disgust. "Don't be ridiculous, man. I have to get back to town. I have important business to take care of and I simply can't sit around waiting for your infernal inspector to turn up. We are leaving first thing in the morning."

George's eyebrows drew together in a ferocious scowl. "May I remind you, sir, that you are addressing a member of the constabulary. I can and will take you into custody if you attempt to leave these premises."

Rodney rolled his eyes, but to Elizabeth's relief muttered, "Oh, very well. I suppose the hospital can manage without me for a few more hours. That's if it's convenient for her ladyship for us to stay."

"Of course," Elizabeth murmured.

"I thought you would see things my way," George said, unsuccessfully hiding a smirk. "I'll see myself out, your ladyship." He moved to the door, pausing to wish everyone a good night before closing it behind him.

The silence in the room, broken only by a few sniffs from Tess, grew uncomfortable.

"I wouldn't worry too much about George," Elizabeth said, getting to her feet. "He tends to jump to conclusions, I'm afraid. I'm sure once the inspector gets here we can clear all this up quickly and you can be on your way. Though I'm afraid it will be more than a few hours. I'd say at least a day or two."

Rodney lifted his hands in a gesture of defeat. "Not much we can do about it now, I suppose."

Daphne sank onto her chair, her face creased in worry. "I'm afraid, Rodney. Things do look rather bad for you and Tess."

"Nonsense," Rodney said gruffly. "You heard what Lady Elizabeth said. The darn chap is jumping to conclusions."

Daphne stared up at her husband. "Well, who else would want to kill Brian? No one but us knew him."

"There was at least one other person," Elizabeth said slowly.

All three Winterhalter's stared at her. "Who?" Rodney demanded.

"The lady Mr. Sutcliffe took to his room." She looked apologetically at Tess, who burst into tears again at this statement.

"Tell us who she was, darling," Daphne said urgently. "It's important that we talk to her. Perhaps she can shed some light on this."

Tess's garbled words, punctuated by her sobs, were unintelligible.

Daphne looked helplessly at Rodney, who muttered, "You're not going to get anything out of her while she's like that. Let her go to bed. We can talk in the morning."

Tess struggled to control her weeping. "I s-said, I don't know who she is."

Rodney muttered something under his breath. "Well, that's that, then."

"No," Daphne cried. "We have to find her and talk to her."

"How did you know Mr. Sutcliffe had a woman in his room?" Elizabeth asked gently.

Tess's answer was muffled, but Elizabeth caught one word.

71

"Sadie? Sadie told you?"

Tess nodded.

"I'll have a word with her first thing in the morning," Elizabeth said, wondering how on earth Sadie had managed to get herself involved in this mess.

Daphne immediately turned to her. "Oh, would you? I would feel so much better if I knew someone intelligent was looking into the matter. I don't trust that constable. He doesn't appear to be all that astute."

"He does seem a little senile for the job," Rodney commented.

Elizabeth sighed. "George, and his partner, Sid, were coaxed out of retirement to take the job, after our constables were called up for military service. I'm afraid they rather regret their circumstances, but they are stuck with it now until the war is over and our younger men return."

"That doesn't give him the excuse to accuse innocent people of murder then hold them against their will." Rodney undid the sash of his smoking jacket and cinched it tighter around his waist. "I shall have a strong word of protest for the inspector when he gets here."

"I should warn you," Elizabeth said, as she crossed to the door, "the inspector is not at all like George. He'll not take a case of murder lightly. I wouldn't expect too much sympathy from him. On the contrary, in fact. He can be quite merciless at times."

Rodney met her gaze without flinching, though Tess received this news with a wail of fright.

"In that case," Rodney said evenly, "we shall just have to answer his questions as best we can."

"Please, your ladyship," Daphne whispered. "Please find out who did this."

Elizabeth sighed. "I'll do my best. That's all I can promise." She bade them all goodnight and left, with the uneasy feeling that this time her best might not be quite good enough.

The next morning Elizabeth confronted Sadie at the breakfast table. Martin had already departed to carry out his "duties," which normally consisted of a morning stroll around the grounds, followed by an inspection of the Great Hall, where he invariably insisted he encountered the late Earl of Wellsborough. After lunch, more often than not, he would retire to the library, from where he could reach the front door within a reasonable amount of time should a visitor summon him with the bell.

Violet was at the stove when Sadie made her appearance in the kitchen. Sunday was Polly's day off, so Elizabeth was alone at the table when the housemaid sat down. She wasted no time in getting to the point.

"Tess tells me you informed her that her friend, Mr. Sutcliffe, entertained a young woman in his room at the Tudor Arms. Is that correct?"

A flush crept across Sadie's cheeks, and she avoided Elizabeth's gaze, pretending instead an avid interest in a piece of dry toast. "I know it was none of my business," she mumbled, "but I thought she should know. I don't like the look of that bloke, and if someone was double-crossing me like that I'd want someone to tell me."

At the stove, Violet turned to send a scathing glare at Sadie. "When are you going to learn to mind your own business, Sadie Buttons? Don't you know you cause more trouble by sticking your nose in where it's not wanted?"

Sadie opened her mouth to argue, but Elizabeth forestalled her. "It's all right, Violet. I just want to ask Sadie a few questions. I prefer that she answer honestly, so I'd rather you didn't interfere."

Violet rolled her eyes at the ceiling and turned her back on them again. The ferocity she used on the unfortunate saucepan in her hand, however, clearly demonstrated her resentment.

Elizabeth pushed a dish of margarine closer to Sadie. "How did you know Mr. Sutcliffe had someone in his room?"

"I saw her, didn't I. See, I took Tess down the pub with me Thursday night 'cos she said she was bored, and the minute we gets inside she recognizes this bloke, Brian. She was really shocked to see him. He'd followed her down from Cambridge just to be with her. She told me her father hated him and didn't want her seeing him. She was afraid Brian would turn up at the wedding and her dad would cause a big scene and throw him out."

Elizabeth winced as Sadie smothered her toast with the margarine. She'd used half her ration on one slice of bread. "So when did you see this woman go into Mr. Sutcliffe's room?"

"It were the next night. Tess had to go to a rehearsal for the wedding so I went to the Arms on me own. I was on me way to the loo and I saw this woman going up the stairs with Brian so I followed them. Tess is me friend, and I always look out for me friends."

"Butt into their business, you mean," Violet muttered.

Ignoring her, Sadie went on. "They were giggling and carrying on when they went inside and shut the door, so I knew they was up to no good."

"Did you recognize the lady?"

Sadie made a sound of disgust. "That weren't no lady, m'm. All done up like a tart, she was."

"But did you recognize her?"

Sadie nodded, her mouth full of toast. "Not until the wedding, though," she said, when she'd swallowed it down. "I didn't know she was Prissy's friend at the time or I might have said something to her."

Elizabeth stared at her. "Fiona? Are you saying it was *Fiona* in that room with Mr. Sutcliffe?"

Sadie grinned. "Shocker, ain't it. Could have blinking knocked me down with a feather when I saw her prancing down the aisle like Lady Muck. That's when I thought I should tell Tess, seeing as how they were bridesmaids together. I was afraid she'd find out from the tart herself, and that would have been even nastier for her."

"I see." Elizabeth leaned back in her chair. She distinctly remembered Fiona saying that Priscilla didn't know the victim. But Fiona didn't mention the fact that she knew him, either. Then again, she probably wouldn't want to advertise the fact that she'd visited the man in his room. Especially in front of Malcolm, who seemed to have a proprietary interest in her.

"I didn't tell Tess before the wedding, of course," Sadie said, reaching for her teacup. "I didn't want them having it out with each other and spoiling everything for Wally and Priscilla. So I waited until we were at the reception before I said anything."

Elizabeth pursed her lips. "Was that before the cake was cut, or after?"

Sadie frowned. "Before. Soon after we first got there, actually. I saw Brian dancing with Tess, then Fiona came in and I knew there'd be trouble so I told Tess right then. She was really upset, so I told her we'd go down the pub as soon as Wally and Prissy left. She was only too happy to get out of there. Practically dragged me out, she did."

"Did she say anything to you about her argument with Mr. Sutcliffe?"

Sadie's eyebrows rose. "No, she didn't. I didn't know she'd said anything to him. What'd she do? Send him packing back to Cambridge?"

Violet turned, a lump of porridge dripping from the wooden spoon in her hand. Her expression mirrored the thought going through Elizabeth's head, but she mercifully kept her silence.

"I'm afraid Mr. Sutcliffe met with an unfortunate accident yesterday," Elizabeth said quietly. "He won't be going anywhere."

Sadie's eyes widened. "He's *dead?*"

"Yes." Elizabeth pushed her chair away from the table and stood. "I'd appreciate it if you wouldn't talk about this to anyone until the inspector has paid us a visit. Most likely he'll want a word with you. Just tell him what you've told me."

Sadie's mouth dropped open. Elizabeth had reached the door before Sadie could speak again. "If the inspector's coming, does that mean he was murdered?"

"With Rita Crumm's wedding knife," Violet said, with unnecessary relish.

Sadie clapped a hand over her mouth. "Does Tess know?" she mumbled behind her fingers.

"Yes." Elizabeth paused to look over her shoulder. "She's extremely upset, naturally. It might be better if you don't mention this to her unless she wants to talk about it."

Sadie nodded. "I'll keep me mouth shut, m'm. Promise."

"That'll be a miracle," Violet muttered, but Elizabeth had closed the door on Sadie's retort. Much as she hated to admit it, things looked black for Tess Winterhalter. It was hard to believe that that fragile creature had taken a knife to her faithless lover, but who knows what a woman was capable of when confronted by such an ugly betrayal.

If Tess was guilty of murder, she hated to think what might happen to the young girl once the inspector got his talons into her. Far better that Elizabeth get a confession out of her first, and then present the result to the inspector herself. Perhaps put in a good word for Tess. She wasn't looking forward to the task. It was so tragic to think that a beautiful young woman could have possibly ruined her entire life.

The Winterhalters had already been served breakfast in the dining room, and Rodney still sat at the table, a newspaper spread out in front of him. He rose as Elizabeth entered the room and waited for her to sit before reseating himself.

"What's the latest news?" Elizabeth asked, as he started to close the newspaper.

"The Germans have retreated from Anzio." He tapped the newspaper with his finger. "It's only a matter of time before Rome will be liberated."

So many times she'd heard positive news from the front, only to hear of a setback soon after. Nowadays, everyone was afraid to hope, even though it seemed the tide might be turning at last. "Do you think we are seeing an end approach?" she asked cautiously, not really expecting a positive answer.

Rodney shook his head. "The Germans are not going to give up that easily. I have a bad feeling that they've got something up their sleeve. If we don't invade Europe soon and get this war over with, we could be in for a good deal of trouble."

Elizabeth sighed. "It's hard to believe the war has dragged on this long. Five years. Who would have thought it could last so long."

Rodney nodded, his bleak expression chilling Elizabeth's bones. "Let's just hope it doesn't last another five years."

The thought was so depressing, she dismissed it from her mind. Besides, right now there was an immediate concern that had to be addressed. She hated to heap more worry on him when he looked so downcast, but the problem had to be faced, and as soon as possible. She took a deep breath. "Rodney, we really need to talk to Tess about what happened to Mr. Sutcliffe."

He seemed to stir himself with an effort, and his face was drawn with anguish when he looked at her. "I know. That damn inspector will be here soon, and I dread the thought of what will happen to her."

"You think she was responsible for his death."

It was a statement rather than a question. He buried his face in his hands for a long moment, then slowly withdrew them. "I knew that wretched man spelled disaster from the first moment I set eyes on him. I tried to warn Tess, but she wouldn't listen to reason. She has my temper . . . I don't know . . ."

"Why don't I talk to her," Elizabeth said, her heart going out to the distraught man. "Where is she?"

"With her mother." He looked up, his eyes dull with pain. "I don't know what Daphne will do. Tess is all we have . . ."

"Let us not assume the worst until we know the truth." Elizabeth rose, bringing Rodney to his feet. "I'll send your wife down to you. I'd rather talk to Tess alone."

He gave her a brief nod. "Very well. I'll think of something to tell her."

She left him alone with his agony, her heart aching.

A few minutes later, she found Tess alone. Daphne, it appeared, had felt the need for some fresh air and was taking a walk. Tess sat fully dressed on the edge of the bed, as if at a loss as to what to do next.

She looked terribly frail and helpless. Her dark eyes seemed to have sunk into her head, and the hollows in her cheeks were even more pronounced.

Elizabeth had to stifle the urge to put her arms around the child and hug her. "I thought we'd have a little chat," she said, when the young girl invited her to sit down. "I know you lied last night, when you said you didn't know who went into Brian's room with him."

A large tear squeezed out of Tess's eye and rolled down her cheek. "I didn't want to talk about it," she whispered.

"Why don't you tell me exactly what happened yesterday," Elizabeth said, as gently as she could.

Tess shook her head. "No, I . . . can't."

"I think you know you'll have to talk about it eventually. If not to me, then to the inspector. He'll want to know everything that happened."

Naked fear turned the girl's face white. "What will happen to me?"

Elizabeth felt a spurt of anger for the events that had caused this young girl so much heartache. It wasn't until that moment she realized just how much she'd been hoping she was wrong about Tess's guilt. "That's something we'll have to worry about later," she said, knowing she could offer little hope. "Just tell me what happened. Did he threaten you?"

"I pushed him," Tess said dully. "He was standing in the doorway of the cellar with his back to the steps. I told him I knew about Fiona being in his room and that I didn't want to see him again. He laughed at me and called me a silly little prude. I lost my temper and picked up the knife."

Elizabeth briefly closed her eyes. When she opened them again she saw tears rolling down the girl's cheeks.

"I would never have hurt him," Tess whispered. "I thought he would have known that. But he grabbed the knife from me and I was afraid he'd . . ." She gulped and pulled in a deep breath. "I pushed him. He sort of stumbled back and I slammed the door and locked it."

Elizabeth studied the tear-stained face. "And you left the key in the lock?"

Tess's brows drew together as if she didn't understand the question. "I don't know. I suppose so. I didn't take it with me." She started crying in earnest. "He just kept pounding and pounding . . . I ran away. He must have fallen down the stairs in the dark and . . . and stabbed himself." She buried her face in her handkerchief while Elizabeth waited for her to recover some control.

After a while she blew her nose, then laid her hands in her lap and continued. "I went back to the main hall to find Sadie. I saw my father and he asked me why I was upset but I couldn't tell him. I just left him and ran outside. Sadie must have seen me and followed me out there. She persuaded me to go back in until after Wally and Aunt Prissy left. Then I changed my clothes and we walked down to the Tudor Arms where she'd left her bicycle." She looked up, tears still rolling down her face. "I never meant to hurt him. Really I didn't."

"It's all right, Tess." Elizabeth got to her feet. "Try not to worry. I have a feeling this is going to work out all right for you, after all."

She left the girl alone, hoping that her hunch was right. Everything depended on how soon she could talk to the people involved, and how long the inspector would be delayed before he arrived to question the Winterhalters. She could only hope she had enough time.

"Are you getting up, Polly?" Edna Barnett's shrill voice echoed up the narrow staircase. "You'll make us late for church if you don't hurry."

Upstairs in her bedroom, Polly pulled a face at her image in the mirror. "I'm coming!" she yelled back, and picked up the silver-backed hairbrush her mother had given her for Christmas. Pulling it through the tangles in her hair, she wished, as she had a thousand times, that she had Marlene's lovely red curls.

She'd tried putting curlers in her own hair, but she only had to look at the rain and her curls would vanish, leaving her with the same boring flat hair.

She'd thought about getting one of those permanent waves, but the idea of being hooked up by a bunch of wires to a machine terrified her. Besides, if she didn't like the results, she'd have to wait for it all to grow out again and that could take years and years.

Polly sighed and put down the brush.

She wished Marlene would come home. She always felt better when her sister was around. Marlene used to cheer her up when she got the miseries. Now there was no one, except Sadie, and she spent most of her time with Joe lately. She missed her dad, too. Even if he was always telling her off.

Polly glanced at the photo of the smiling man in navy uniform that stood on her dressing table. It had been so long since she'd seen Pa she'd almost forgotten what he looked like.

"Polly? *Polly!* Get down here this minute. If I have to come up there and get you, my girl, I'll box your blinking ears."

"I'm coming! Keep your bloody wig on." Polly jumped to her feet, grabbed her handbag and her jacket, and stomped from the room. She was wearing her best high-heeled platform sandals and on the way down the stairs she turned her ankle.

Limping into the kitchen, she felt like crying. Nothing was going right anymore. Nothing at all. It didn't seem worth going to church. God didn't listen to her prayers anyway. She'd prayed that Sam would come back from America and tell her he'd missed her too much to live without her. She'd prayed that Marlene would be sent back to England. She'd prayed for the war to end and all the soldiers to come back home. None of it had happened. None of it.

"Take that miserable look off your face," Edna Barnett ordered, as the two of them set off for the long walk to the church. "What has a young girl like you got to be so gloomy about?"

"Everything," Polly mumbled. If only Sam hadn't gone and left her. Summer was coming, and she could have looked forward to picnics and rides in the Jeep and walks along the cliffs and cuddling in the car park behind the Tudor Arms. She got a pain in her chest every time she thought about him. When was it going to stop hurting? That's what she'd pray for today. To stop hurting when she thought about Sam. Or maybe even to stop thinking about Sam.

No, she couldn't do that. The thought of banishing him from her mind altogether was too terrible to contemplate. Even when she'd been going out with Ray, which turned out to be a bad mistake, she'd still thought about Sam. It was as if she kept him in a small piece of her heart, so that whenever she felt sad and lonely, he'd still be there to keep her company. Even if it did still hurt.

Engrossed in her thoughts, she failed to hear what her mother said, until Edna barked, "Did you hear me?"

Polly jumped. "What?"

"I said, I've got something that might cheer you up."

Without much enthusiasm, Polly muttered, "What is it?" Probably a bag of broken biscuits that Ma had bought off ration. Ma always thought that sweets could cure the worst misery. A cup of tea and a biscuit. That was Ma's answer to everything.

"There's a letter came for you yesterday."

Polly stopped short in the road and stared at her mother's back. "A letter? Is it from Sam?"

"No, it's not from America."

Polly lost some of her enthusiasm. "Who's it from? Why didn't you tell me before?"

"Because it came while we were at the wedding, and then you didn't come home until after I was in bed." Edna paused to look back at her daughter. "I don't know what your father would say if he knew you was coming home late like that. Staying down that pub all hours of the night."

"I wasn't at the pub. I was riding me bicycle along the cliffs."

Edna's face registered shock. "How many times have I told you it's dangerous to be riding along the cliffs at night without lights? Have you forgotten that a young lady died from falling over them cliffs?"

"She didn't fall; she was pushed," Polly said. "Anyhow, who's the letter from. Marlene?"

Edna shook her head.

"Pa?"

"No, I don't know who it's from. I thought it was Marlene at first 'cos it's got a foreign stamp on it. I think it's from Italy, but it's not her writing."

Polly felt a spasm of fear. "What if something's happened to her and someone's writing to tell us about it?"

"They don't write letters," Edna said calmly, though her face looked pale in the sunlight. "They send telegrams. Didn't you send letters to a bunch of soldiers over there?"

Polly blinked, still shaken by the possibility of Marlene being hurt. "Soldiers? Oh, yes! I did! It's been so long I forgot."

Edna started walking away. "Come on, if we don't hurry we'll be late."

"Why didn't you give it to me this morning?" Polly demanded, hurrying as

89

best she could on her high heels to catch up with her mother.

"Because you were taking so long to get ready for church." Edna quickened her steps as Polly drew level. "I knew if I gave it to you then you'd take even longer."

Polly didn't answer. Her mind was buzzing with questions. A few months earlier, she and Sadie had collected letters from villagers and sent them to Marlene who'd promised to give them out to servicemen desperate for news from home. Polly had written a long letter herself, but had never really expected an answer.

She felt a little skip of excitement as she thought about the letter waiting for her. A letter from a mysterious stranger. Who was he? What was he like? How old was he? Where was his home? She could hardly wait now, to read it.

All through the service she kept thinking about it, and had to be nudged twice by her mother when she failed to stand up for the hymns.

At long last the sermon was over, and it wasn't until she was outside the church again that she realized she'd forgotten to pray for the pain to go away when she thought about Sam. That was because she hadn't thought about Sam at all, she realized with a shock.

That upset her at first, but then she started thinking about the letter again and her spirits soared. She couldn't wait to read the letter and find out all about the person who'd sent it. Things were looking up. Life could still be exciting after all.

Chapter 5

When Elizabeth went in search of the Winterhalters, Violet informed her that Daphne had not returned from her walk and Rodney had gone to look for her. Since Elizabeth barely had time to get to the church on her motorcycle in time for the service, she was forced to wait until later before she could talk to Tess's parents.

She'd hoped to see Earl that morning; he often joined her for the Sunday service, but she could see no sign of his dark head as she entered the church. Aware that people were discussing the death of Brian Sutcliffe, she avoided conversation with anyone and left hurriedly as soon as the service was over.

She arrived back at the manor in time to see both Daphne and Rodney strolling up the driveway. The sight of them greatly relieved her. She'd been rather worried that something might have happened to Daphne. Which just proved how easy it was to jump to conclusions.

She waited until the Winterhalters had settled themselves in the library before going in to see them. They both looked up as she entered, with identical expressions of dread on their faces. She hurried to reassure them.

"I've talked to Tess," she told them, "and I don't think she is responsible for the death of Brian Sutcliffe."

Both parents uttered exclamations, though Rodney looked far more relieved than his wife.

He rose to his feet, one hand raking through his hair. "Did she tell you what happened?"

"Yes, she did." Elizabeth sat on her favorite armchair by the fireplace and smiled at Daphne, who still looked stricken. "I really can't go into it now, as I have many more questions to ask and people to talk to before we can come to any conclusions. As soon as I know something for certain I'll let you know."

"Do you have any idea who might have killed Brian?" Daphne asked, one hand clutching her throat.

"Not at present, no." Elizabeth stood. "But I can assure you I'll do everything in my power to ferret out the truth."

"Well, if there's anything we can do to help . . ." Rodney walked to the door with her. "I can't thank you enough, Lady Elizabeth. As you can imagine, my wife and I have been out of our minds with worry. I only hope we can solve this mess before the inspector gets here and jumps to the wrong conclusion, as P.C. Dalrymple did."

Heartily agreeing with that sentiment, Elizabeth left them alone and headed for the kitchen. She was eager to have her lunch and then get out of the manor for a while, in order to clear her mind. A brisk stroll across the downs with her two dogs, Gracie and George, bounding along by her side was just what she needed to organize her thoughts.

It wasn't until she was tramping through the long grass that she allowed herself to think about Earl. He'd been absent a lot lately, and he seemed preoccupied. Which usually meant something big was brewing at the base. Talk of the Allied invasion of Europe had been the main topic of news lately, both in the newspaper and on the wireless. Speculation, of course. No one knew when or even if it would eventually take place.

One thing Elizabeth did know: if there was to be an invasion, Earl would be in the thick of it. The troops landing on the beaches would need air support. Undoubtedly that was the reason he'd been sent back to his base in England. Something else was just as certain. She wouldn't know he'd gone until it was over. One way or another.

The fear that always hovered in the back of her mind surged to the forefront. To lose him now, just when the path ahead of them appeared to be offering a chance for happiness, would be too terrible to bear. She was devastated when he left England the year before, but there had always been a faint hope to cling to, a chance that she would see him again someday. To have him come back to her, only to lose him forever, would destroy her completely. No, it was too awful to even think about.

Her eyes misted with tears, she didn't recognize the figure standing on the edge of the cliffs at first. The dogs, however, had no such reservations and were leaping about with joyous whines and yaps that left no doubt in her mind.

It was as if he'd materialized out of her thoughts, and for a moment she was too full of emotion to speak as she reached him.

"I was on my way back to the manor," he said, holding out his hand. "I saw you across the downs and figured I'd wait for you here." He'd parked the Jeep on the grass verge a few yards behind him. The dogs scrambled into it, their noses busily sniffing out unfamiliar smells.

Smiling, Elizabeth put her hand in his. "I was just thinking about you."

She'd said it lightly, but the glow in his eyes intensified. "I'm happy to hear that." He squeezed her hand and let it go. "You want to walk?"

She fell into step beside him as he started back across the cliffs away from the manor.

"I don't feel like going back to my quarters just yet," he said, linking her arm through his. "I want to be out here in the sun and the fresh air on a nice, normal, Sunday afternoon. For a while I want to forget everything and everyone and relax with my best girl."

Something about the way he said it brought a chill to her heart. "You're going away," she said, her voice flat with misery.

He glanced at her, his expression hard to read. "Not as far as I know. Not yet, anyway."

"Then what is it?"

He halted and pulled her around to face him. "You know I can't tell you anything specific. It's just that I might not be able to spend much time with you for the next week or two. Things are heating up, and I'll be pretty tied up for a while. I've just got time to pick up my stuff this afternoon and I'm heading back to the base."

The hollow in her stomach grew larger. "The invasion?"

"Elizabeth . . ."

"I know. You can't tell me." She pulled away from him, determined not to let him see her fear. "Well, then," she added stiffly, "we'll just have to talk about something else. What do you think these little pink flowers are called?" She turned her back and walked away from him, gesturing fiercely at the clump of wildflowers growing alongside the railings that lined the cliff path. "They come back every year and no one seems to know their name."

"Dammit, Elizabeth!" He caught up with her, seized her arms, and turned her to face him again. "You know I'd tell you if I could."

Struggling to keep the tears at bay, she muttered, "Yes, I do. It's just that it's so hard, not knowing. I try not to think about it, but every time I pick up a newspaper . . ." She looked up at him, helpless to continue.

The look in his eyes cut off her breath. "You know, Lady Elizabeth Hartleigh

Compton, you sure make it hard for me to keep my promise."

"Then don't." She didn't know she'd said the words out loud until she saw his face change. Even if she could take them back, she knew she wouldn't. Yes, he was right. They should wait. His divorce wasn't finalized yet. Officially he was still married. Protocol demanded they keep their distance from each other, at least until he was a free man.

Right at that minute, however, none of that seemed to matter. No one was around to see them, and heaven only knew when she would be alone with him again. If ever. No, she would not take back the words.

She waited for what seemed an eternity before he moved. She wondered if he'd understood, but then he pulled her into his arms and covered her mouth with his. It seemed as if everything — the trees, dogs, birds, the grass, the ocean, the sun, and the salty breeze, all of it — disappeared into one soundless moment in time. *So this,* she thought with a sense of wonder, *this is what being in love is really like.*

Polly flew up the stairs so fast she tripped at the top and went sprawling onto the landing. The carpet scraped her knee and she winced. Another flipping ladder to ruin her stockings.

Edna's voice screeched up the stairs. "What are you doing up there? You sound like a herd of elephants."

Polly pulled a face and scrambled to her feet. "I tripped, that's all." The precious letter had crumpled in her hand, and she smoothed it out.

"It's those blasted high heels you wear. You'll break your neck in those, my girl. You mark my words."

Having heard the dire warning too many times to count, Polly ignored it and limped into the bedroom. With a flick of her foot she kicked off one sandal, then the other, and sank onto the bed.

She stared at her address written in an untidy scrawl across the envelope. Just above her name was a smudge of dirt, as if it had been splashed with mud. Tense with excitement, she stared at it, wondering where the writer had been when he wrote the letter.

There was one way to find out. Very carefully, hardly daring to breathe, she opened the flap with her thumb and drew out the flimsy pages.

There were three pages altogether, covered in the same scrawl, which at times was hard to read. She skimmed through it at first, skipping the newsy parts to get to something personal. She found it halfway down the last page.

You sound like a really nice girl, Polly. I hope you'll go on writing to me. I'd love to hear from you again. If you can, send me a photograph. I'd like to know what you look like. I'll send you one of me in the next letter. Until then, I'll be thinking about you and looking forward to hearing from you again. Yours sincerely, Pte. Tom Reynolds.

Polly pressed the letter against her heart for a moment. His name was Tom! He was nineteen. Only three years older than her. He lived in Surrey, near London, and he liked dancing and football. Well, she wasn't much of a dancer, and she never saw a football match, but that was something that could be worked on later. *Tom.* She tried it out loud. "Tom and Polly Reynolds." Yes, it sounded good.

She went back and read the letter again, more slowly this time, taking in every word. He sounded well-educated. That worried her for a moment. She hoped he didn't talk posh like Tess Winterhalter. That would put a block on it from the start. Oh, well. She'd worry about that later.

She leapt from the bed and opened the top drawer of her dressing table. The cardboard cigar box that held her photographs was tucked underneath a pile of undies. She drew it out and opened it, then spread all the photographs out on the bed.

This one made her look too young. This one made her look ugly. In this one her hair was a mess, and this one was taken on a windy day and half her hair was wrapped around her face. None of them made her look like a film star.

Finally, in desperation, she settled on one that didn't look too bad. It was taken in the summer, by Sam. She was standing by her bicycle and laughing at something Sam had said. The blue and white frock she had on that day was one of her favorites, with its little puffy sleeves and a full skirt.

For a moment tears pricked at her eyelids when she remembered that day. It was taken before the accident that had messed up Sam's face. He looked so handsome back then. She thought she'd never seen anyone so handsome. Not even Clark Gable or Errol Flynn was as handsome as her Sam.

She stared at the photograph in her hand. She couldn't send this to a stranger.

Not if it meant explaining about Sam. She looked at the pile of discarded photographs lying on the bed, then at the one in her hand again. Confused and uncertain, she reached for Tom's letter and read it again.

He'd never know Sam took it. She'd never tell him. Not even if they ended up getting married and living the rest of their lives together.

With a long sigh she gathered up the rest of the photographs and put them back in the box. After tucking it away in the drawer, she fetched her writing pad and pencil and started her letter to Tom. When she was finished, she tucked the photograph inside the letter, sealed the envelope, and propped it up on her dressing table. Tomorrow she'd take it to the post office.

At the door to her bedroom she paused and looked back. The envelope stared back at her, full of promise and exciting unknowns. "Good-bye, Sam," she said softly, and closed the door.

Elizabeth was quite breathless when Earl finally let her go. Breathless and dizzy and feeling ridiculously young and shy. She couldn't look at him, and instead pretended to be anxious about the dogs, both of whom were chasing butterflies, blissfully oblivious of the earth-shattering moment that had just taken place.

He still held her hands, and she sought frantically in her mind for something sensible to say. Anything that would break the forbidden spell that bonded them. In desperation, she said the first words that popped into her mind. "I'm supposed to be investigating a murder."

Earl's voice sounded strange when he answered. "Elizabeth, you have the darndest knack for deflating a man's ego."

Appalled at her insensitivity, she stared up at him. "Oh, Earl, I didn't mean . . ."

His chuckle both surprised and relieved her. "It's all right. You're being sensible and practical and all the things I'm supposed to be and can't be right now. And you're right. This isn't a good idea. I guess we just got caught up in the moment."

For some reason, his words disheartened her. "It's not that I didn't enjoy it," she murmured. "Quite the opposite, in fact. It's just that —"

Gently he laid a finger on her lips. "I know. You don't have to explain. There'll be a right time for us. We just have to be patient, that's all."

Her smile was an effort. "Sometimes it's hard."

"Tell me about it." He lifted her hand and pressed his lips to her fingers. "Come on, let's corral George and Gracie and give them a ride back to the manor. They love to ride in the Jeep."

Sad that her short, blissful time with him was ending so rapidly, she watched him whistle to the dogs. They came at once and, tails wagging, followed him back to the Jeep. She trailed behind them, committing to memory the picture of man and dogs, happy and carefree in each other's company. It would be all she had while he was away.

Arriving back at the manor, he pulled up in the courtyard and turned to her. The dogs leapt from the Jeep and disappeared around the corner of the ancient building. "I guess this is good-bye for a while," he said, smiling down at her.

It was hard to smile back. "You take care of yourself," she said, striving to keep her tone light.

"You, too." His grin faded. "Stay out of harm's way, Elizabeth. I won't always be around to help out."

"I know." She grasped his hand in both of hers. "Don't worry about me, Earl. I promise I won't do anything foolish. Just concentrate on coming safely back to me."

"You've got a deal." He touched her cheek with his free hand. "So long, sweetheart."

She caught her breath. It was the first time he'd used the endearment. It was something else to cling to in the dark hours ahead. She could not say good-bye. It was too final. She'd never been able to say it to him. Even when she'd thought he was leaving her life forever. "Until we meet again," she said, adding inwardly, *my love.*

Instead of waiting for him to help her down from the Jeep, she scrambled out on her own. The last she heard of him was the roar of his engine as he drove off to the back of the manor.

Rather than wait the eternity it took Martin to open the front door for her, she made her way through the greenhouses to the kitchen door. Violet was putting dishes away when she entered and looked up in surprise.

"I thought you were taking the dogs for a walk," she said, sliding the last dinner plate onto the pile in the cupboard.

"I was." Elizabeth glanced at the clock. "I have to get down to the village hall now. Bessie is going back there this afternoon to finish cleaning up and I want to talk to her."

Violet peered at her over her shoulder. "About the murder?"

"We don't know if it's a murder yet," Elizabeth pointed out.

"From what I understand, some poor bugger was lying dead on the floor with a knife in his chest. I daresay he didn't put it there himself."

"It could have been an accident. He could have fallen with the knife in his hand."

Violet turned all the way around. "And what would he be doing in the cellar with a knife in the first place?"

Elizabeth smiled. "Don't worry, Violet. I'll find out what happened. I usually do."

"That's what worries me. You always seem to end up in trouble yourself when you start going around asking questions like that."

"With so many people worrying about me," Elizabeth said, as she headed for the door, "how can I possibly get into trouble?" She closed the door behind her, before Violet could answer.

A few minutes later she halted her motorcycle in front of the village hall, just as Bessie emerged carrying a huge box. By the way she staggered as she reached the gate, Elizabeth could tell the poor woman's load was too heavy for her.

Elizabeth climbed off her motorcycle with as much haste as decorum allowed and hurried to help Bessie squeeze through the gate.

"Thank you, your ladyship," Bessie said, panting with exertion. "I thought I was going to drop it. Really I did."

"I do hope you're not expecting to carry this all the way back to the Bake Shop." Elizabeth grasped one edge of the box.

"Well, I was going to try." Bessie looked doubtfully at the motorcycle. "I carried it down here."

"But it's uphill all the way back." Elizabeth shifted the weight of the box against her hip. "What's in here, anyway?"

"China. The ladies from the Housewives League brought glasses and plates, and I brought the cups and saucers from the tea shop."

"Oh, my." Elizabeth wavered, then said cautiously, "I could run them up in the sidecar of my motorcycle, if you like."

Bessie's face shone with relief. "Oh, would you? Thank you, m'm. I'd be ever so grateful, really I would. I still have to pack up the linens and the cutlery."

"Right. Let's get this in . . . *here*." Elizabeth delivered the last word on a groan as they heaved the box into the tiny sidecar.

"It only just fits," she said, as she wiggled the box to make sure it was secure.

"Thank you, m'm. I'll get back inside and finish clearing up. Some of the ladies came to help me and I don't want to leave them working on their own."

Elizabeth climbed aboard the motorcycle, kicked the engine to life, and tucked her pleated skirt securely under her knees. "I'll be back in a few minutes," she said, shouting over the roar of her engine. "I'd like a word with you before you leave."

Bessie nodded, waved her hand, and scurried back to the hall.

Mindful of her precious cargo, Elizabeth rode cautiously up the hill to the High Street. Housewives loaded down with heavy shopping bags waved to her as she passed, and she nodded in response, too anxious to raise a hand from the handlebars. It was with a sigh of relief that she finally braked to a halt in front of Bessie's Bake Shop.

Two of Bessie's assistants rushed out to help her unload the cumbersome box and wrestle it into the shop. The heavenly aroma of freshly baked bread and buns was almost irresistible, but anxious to talk to Bessie before she left the hall, Elizabeth reluctantly returned to her motorcycle.

To her surprise, she saw George and his long-suffering partner Sid hovering around the vehicle when she emerged onto the street. The two constables were deep in conversation, which they broke off the minute Elizabeth arrived within earshot.

They greeted her in unison, and just a little too hastily. She knew at once they had been talking about her. "Am I parked in the wrong place?" she asked, knowing perfectly well that unlike North Horsham, there were no restrictions in the High Street in Sitting Marsh.

"No, no, your ladyship," Sid hastened to assure her. "It was just that me and George —"

"Were discussing the weather," George interrupted loudly.

Sid sent him a puzzled look. "No, we weren't. You were saying as how —"

"Don't you have something urgent to do at the station?" George said, glowering at Sid.

Sid raised his eyebrows. "It's *Sunday,*" he said, his voice rising in protest.

"Ho, ho," George said, sounding a little like a bored Father Christmas. "A policeman's work is never done, isn't that right, your ladyship?"

"Quite," Elizabeth murmured. She knew

quite well it was only a matter of time before Sid blurted out what George was trying so hard to keep quiet. "I admire dedicated men such as you two. Always on duty. Makes one feel so terribly secure."

George eyed her warily, while Sid beamed. "That's so nice of you to say, Lady Elizabeth. I was just saying to George, I was —"

George loudly cleared his throat. "I'm sure her ladyship has better things to do this afternoon than stand around listening to your idle chatter, Sid."

"Not at all," Elizabeth said brightly. "I'm always interested in what Sid has to say. He can be so terribly informative at times."

"Don't I bloody know it," George muttered.

Sid preened. "I do me best, your ladyship."

Elizabeth smiled at him. "You certainly seemed concerned about something just now. I do hope I don't have a flat tire."

Apparently oblivious of George's fierce glare, Sid's hearty laugh rang out. "Oh, no, m'm. Nothing like that. George was just saying he hoped the inspector got here and arrested the murderer before you got in the way again."

This time George's frantic coughing failed to cover up Sid's words. Elizabeth gave him a frosty look. "Why, George, I thought you always appreciated my efforts to solve your cases for you."

George's face turned beet red, and he ran a finger around the collar of his shirt as if it were choking him. "Yes, I do. Most of the time, that is. But this time we know who the murderer is, and I wouldn't like to see you go to all that trouble of asking everyone questions like you always do when it ain't . . . isn't necessary." He coughed again, then added as an afterthought, "Your ladyship."

Elizabeth fixed him with a stern eye. "You know who murdered Brian Sutcliffe?"

"Yes, m'm."

"Then perhaps you'd be so kind as to inform me, just so I won't get in your way."

George looked as if he were about to cry. "I can't do that, your ladyship. You know I can't."

"Course you can," Sid said cheerfully. "You know who it is, Lady Elizabeth. It's the chap what's staying at the manor, isn't it. Mr. Rodney Winterhalter is the one what killed Mr. Sutcliffe. Isn't that right, George?"

Chapter 6

Polly stood at the front door of the Manor House and tugged on the bell pull for the third time. She was fast losing her patience. She was dying to show her letter to Sadie, and that old fool, Martin, was taking his blinking time opening the door for her.

If the kitchen door wasn't locked she could get in that way, which is the way she usually went in. But on Sundays Violet took the afternoon off and locked the kitchen door, so here she was, hopping up and down waiting for Martin to wake up and let her in.

She was about to hang on the bell rope again when she heard the first bolt sliding back. At last. What the bloomin' heck had he been doing? Another bolt scraped open, then the huge iron key grated in the lock. Two more bolts to go and the latch to lift. All she could hope was that he didn't fall asleep again before he got them all open.

At long last the door inched open a crack. Her impatience exhausted, Polly gave the door a shove. To her dismay, she heard a muffled exclamation, then a thud.

The old boy must have fallen down again. He was always falling down these days. It was a wonder he didn't break his bloomin' neck.

She pushed the door, but it refused to budge any further. Getting anxious now, she put her mouth up to the crack. "Martin? Are you all right?"

To her relief, his crusty voice answered her. "No, I am most definitely not all right. The blessed door just attacked me."

She sighed. "Did you hurt yourself?"

"Not at all. I bounce off doors and land flat on my back for the pure fun of it."

"Can you get up?"

"If I could get up," Martin said peevishly, "do you think I'd still be lying here like a beached whale? Who are you, anyway?"

"It's Polly." She waited, and when no response seemed forthcoming, added helpfully, "Polly Barnett."

"I am not acquainted with Polly Barnett."

"Yes, you are," Polly said, rolling her eyes skyward. "I'm Lady Elizabeth's assistant."

"Lady Elizabeth is not at home, so she doesn't need your assistance."

"I didn't come here to work." Polly was fast losing her patience again. "I came to see Sadie."

"Miss Buttons is finishing her chores. At

least she's supposed to be finishing her chores. Heaven knows what the dratted girl gets up to when no one is watching her. I never did trust that hussy."

Polly pushed the door again, but Martin's body still prevented it from opening.

Martin's voice rose a notch. "If you'd stop hammering me with the door I might consider making an attempt to get back on to my feet."

"Sorry." She waited. And waited. "Are you getting up?" she asked, when there seemed no sign of movement from the other side of the door.

"In a moment. I'm studying the ceiling. I think it needs a good scrubbing."

"Something needs a good scrubbing," Polly muttered under her breath. Deciding that drastic measures needed to be taken, she grasped the bell rope again and gave it a hearty tug. A loud clang rang out and echoed from within the hallway.

"Who's there?" Martin called out.

Polly rolled her eyes again and heaved a heavy sigh. "It's still Polly Barnett."

"Well, what are you doing dithering about out there? Come in, come in."

"I would if I could bloody get in," Polly muttered. She jumped as the door suddenly swung open.

Martin stood in the doorway, his half dozen silver hairs standing on end. He peered at her over the gold rims of his glasses. "Did you say something?"

"I said thank you very much, Martin." Polly darted past him before he could delay her any longer. She heard him muttering something as she raced up the stairs to the great hall, but paid no attention. All she could think about now was showing her letter to Sadie.

She found the housemaid in the great hall. Sadie was about halfway down, dusting the suit of armor that stood between the tall windows. As Polly drew near, her feet soundless on the thick carpet, she heard Sadie talking softly to herself.

"There you go, me old matey. Now you're all spruced up, how about giving me a ride on that white horse of yours? I could do with some excitement in me life."

Polly grinned as she came up behind the unsuspecting girl. "You won't get much excitement out of that lump of metal," she said loudly.

Sadie screeched and spun around, but instead of looking at Polly, she seemed to be staring wide-eyed at something behind Polly's back.

Remembering the ghosts that had been sighted in the great hall, Polly's skin prickled with fear. She twisted around to look behind her, the echo of her shriek reaching the far end of the hall. All she could see were the portraits of generations of ancestors staring down from the towering walls.

"Cor blimey, Polly," Sadie said, wiping her brow with the duster. "Whatcha go and do that for? You nearly scared me out of me knickers."

Annoyed with herself, Polly muttered, "Well, you scared me, too. I thought you'd seen a ghost. What were you looking at, anyhow?"

"I dunno." Sadie shook out the duster, sending a cloud of dust back over the suit of armor. "I jumped when you spoke and swung around to look. Then you screamed and made me jump again. I s'pose it's hearing about that bloke what got murdered at the wedding. Given me the jitters, it has."

Polly stared at her. "What bloke?"

"Brian. The bloke I told you about. The one what followed Tess down from Cambridge. They found him in the cellar. Someone stuck a knife in his chest."

"Oh, heck!" Polly shook her head in disbelief. "How awful. Nice looking bloke he was, too. Who would do that to him?"

To Polly's surprise, Sadie looked up and down the hall as if worried someone might be there. "Well, don't say nothing to no one, but I think Tess might have done it. I didn't say nothing to you before, but I saw that tart, Fiona, go into Brian's room at the pub, and when I told Tess about it she blew her top."

"So that's what he did," Polly murmured, remembering her conversation with Tess at the pub.

"I think she went after him with the knife and he fell down the cellar steps." Sadie started dusting the armor again. "Can't say I blame her. I'd have done the same if some bloke did that to me."

"You'd have killed him?"

"Nah. I'd just frighten the living daylights out of the bugger." Sadie looked at her over her shoulder. "Per'aps that's what Tess did. Per'aps she didn't mean to kill him. It could have been an accident."

Polly frowned. "I can't believe Tess would do something like that. Besides, she was talking about him down at the pub last night. I'd swear she didn't know he was dead then."

"Maybe she didn't know she'd killed him until someone told her."

"Poor Tess. She must be so frightened and upset."

"Yeah." Sadie gave the duster a final flourish. "Lady Elizabeth said she was in a terrible tizz." She turned to face her friend. "Anyhow, what are you doing here on a Sunday?"

Forgetting Tess's problems for the time being, Polly pulled the letter from her pocket and waved it in Sadie's face. "Look what came in the post yesterday."

Sadie took it from her and studied the envelope. "From Marlene?"

"No, silly. From a soldier. You know, the ones what wanted letters from home?"

Sadie's face brightened. "Oh, them! You heard from one? What's he like? I wish I'd sent one now."

Polly stared at her in surprise. "I thought you were daffy about Joe."

"Nah, Joe's nice, but he's so slow. I like 'em with a bit more pizzaaazz."

She'd sort of drawled it and wriggled her hips, making Polly laugh. "Why don't you write a letter then," she said. "Come over my house tonight and we'll write it together."

"Great idea! I'll be there."

"I'll send it to Tom and ask if he has a friend that wants to write back to you."

"His name is Tom? Can I read it?"

Polly watched as Sadie scanned the lines Tom had written. At last she raised her head and grinned at Polly. "He sounds a right charmer, don't he. Wonder what he looks like?"

"We'll find out when I get his next letter." Polly took the letter back and tucked it in her pocket. "I'm sending him a photograph of me tomorrow."

Tomorrow. She felt a little jump of excitement. Tomorrow her letter would be on the way to Tom, and who knows what would come out of it. Now she couldn't wait to get a letter back from him, and a photograph. If only time would go by faster. "I wish," she said, as she walked with Sadie back to the stairs, "that I had a crystal ball that would tell me what's going to happen in the future."

"You're not the only one." Sadie paused at the top of the stairs. "And I wouldn't mind betting that right now, Tess Winterhalter is thinking the same thing as well."

Elizabeth stared in dismay at George's furious face. "What, may I ask, had led you to the conclusion that Rodney Winterhalter killed Brian Sutcliffe?"

George smoothed out his glare, which

had been directed at Sid, and said stiffly, "I'm not at liberty to discuss it, your ladyship. You know how it is."

"Yes, I do know how it is." Elizabeth tied her scarf more firmly under her chin. "I know very well that misplaced speculation can result in some unpleasant consequences. For all concerned."

George lifted his chin. "Certain facts have come to my attention, from which I have deduced that Mr. Winterhalter had both motive and opportunity."

"What facts?" Elizabeth demanded bluntly.

George cleared his throat. "Your ladyship —"

"I shall find out sooner or later, George. You will save us both a great deal of trouble if you simply tell me now."

George let out his breath in frustration.

"He was seen leaving the kitchen round about the time of the murder," Sid said.

George sent him another withering look. "Just remember he told you that, m'm. Not me."

"Who saw Mr. Winterhalter leave the kitchen?"

"It were Nellie Smith," George answered, beating Sid to the punch. "And that's me last word on the subject." He sent Sid a meaningful look. "And yours."

"Well, thank you. Both of you." Elizabeth straddled the saddle of her motorcycle. "Now, if you'll excuse me, I have my own investigation to conduct."

"The inspector won't like you interfering, m'm," George warned.

"The inspector," Elizabeth said, rising up to kick start the engine, "will thank me when I save him, and you, George, from a grave miscarriage of justice."

"If you find out anything, your ladyship, you're under an obligation —"

The rest of George's words were drowned out by the roar of the motorcycle's engine. Smiling and waving, Elizabeth soared off down the street, narrowly missing a startled housewife scurrying across the road.

No matter what George thought, Elizabeth told herself as she rode down the hill, she would not believe Rodney had stabbed Brian Sutcliffe. He had been too distraught at the thought of his daughter possibly being involved.

Nor did she believe that Tess had killed her lover. But she intended to make quite certain of that before she tackled the other people on her list.

Arriving back at the village hall, she parked her motorcycle and cut the engine.

She had taken longer than she had intended to deliver Bessie's china to the shop. She could only hope Bessie was still inside.

To her relief, not only was Bessie still there, but several members of the Housewives League stood about, apparently finishing up the cleanup. She spotted Nellie in the group, and headed over to her, intent on speaking to the young lady before she left.

Elizabeth wasted no time in coming to the point when she drew Nellie aside. "I understand you saw Rodney Winterhalter leaving the kitchen yesterday afternoon about the time of the murder," she said.

Nellie looked apprehensive. "I didn't want to get no one in trouble, your ladyship, but George did ask and I had to say what I saw."

Elizabeth nodded. "It's all right, Nellie. What exactly did you see?"

"Well, it were a little while before all that fuss about the missing knife. I seen Mr. Winterhalter rushing out of the kitchen, and he looked really upset about something. I wondered at the time what he was doing in there, but then Florrie went in to get the knife and came running out again to say it were missing and, well, you heard the rest."

"Did you see where Mr. Winterhalter went after he left the kitchen?"

Nellie shook her head. "I was too busy helping Florrie look for the knife."

"Very well. Thank you, Nellie." Elizabeth smiled at the worried-looking girl. "You did the right thing. Please don't give it another thought."

"Yes, m'm." Still looking concerned, Nellie went back to join the group that was now stacking chairs against the walls.

Bessie seemed to have disappeared, and Elizabeth hurried into the kitchen, hoping to find her in there. Pleased to find her alone, Elizabeth complimented her on the fine job she had done with the wedding.

"There's just one thing I'd like to ask you," she said, when Bessie thanked her. "You said yesterday that you found the key to the cellar in a milk jug. Where exactly was it standing when Florrie picked it up to empty it?"

Bessie pointed to a table by the wall. "It were on there, m'm."

Elizabeth walked over to the table, followed by an anxious Bessie. "On here?" She pointed to the table.

"Yes, m'm. Right here." Bessie patted the table.

Elizabeth raised her gaze to the shelf

123

above the table. "Were you using this shelf for anything yesterday?"

"No, m'm, we weren't. It's in an awkward spot, isn't it. We'd have to have really long arms to reach up there across the table."

"Which is probably why the key fell off," Elizabeth murmured.

Bessie poked her head forward. "What did you say, your ladyship?"

"No matter." Elizabeth looked around. "Everything looks spick and span, Bessie. You and the rest of the Housewives League provided a lovely wedding for Priscilla and Wally. I know they must be so grateful to you all."

Bessie's smile was radiant. "We were all happy to do it, m'm. Everyone likes Prissy, and Captain Carbunkle is a good sort. They'll be happy together, I know." She glanced over her shoulder as if to make sure they were alone. "Can't imagine our Prissy having a friend like that Fiona. Not a bit alike, are they. Someone said Fiona married an old bloke for his money and when he died he left her a fortune. Bit of a fly-by-night if you ask me. I wouldn't have thought Prissy would be that friendly with someone like that."

Elizabeth wondered if Bessie had heard

about Fiona's indiscretion with the murdered man, but thought better about asking her. "Well, they hadn't seen each other in thirty years. I'm sure they both must have changed in that time. Anyway, I must be off. Violet will be getting supper and I don't want to be late. Oh, before I go, could you let me have the address of the photographer. Dickie Muggins, I believe?"

"Yes, m'm. I have it right here in my handbag. Just a minute." Bessie bustled across the kitchen to a tall cupboard and opened it. She came bag with a large black handbag tucked under her arm. "He's a good photographer, m'm. I've seen some of his photographs. Lovely they are. He's a bit of a fusspot, and some people make fun of him for it, but he knows what he's doing all right, I'll say that for him."

Thank you, Bessie." Elizabeth took the neatly inscribed card from Bessie and tucked it in her pocket. "I'll let you have it back next time I visit the tea shop."

"Oh, no need, your ladyship. I have some more. Dickie's mother gave them to me. He's just started his business, and he's looking for more clients. He'll be pleased to hear from you, I'm sure."

Elizabeth rather doubted that. She

wasn't looking to hire him, but merely ask him a few questions. She didn't see the need to tell Bessie that, however.

She left the hall deep in thought and returned to the manor, convinced now that Tess had not killed Brian Sutcliffe. The girl had no reason to lie about leaving the key in the lock. Moreover, if she was telling the truth she'd heard Brian pounding on the door when she left, which meant he was still alive at that point.

Someone else must have removed the key from the cellar door. It seemed reasonable to assume that that person did so to delay the discovery of the body. Someone could have heard Brian pounding on the door, unlocked it, and confronted an angry man with a knife in his hand. What then? Reacted without thinking and pushed him down the stairs, causing him to fall on the knife, as Tess had surmised? Or had someone taken the opportunity to get rid of a man who was causing more trouble than was bearable?

A milk jug full of milk seemed an odd place to hide a key. But what if the killer intended to hide it on the shelf? Then, unnerved and in a hurry to leave, stretched out to reach the shelf and fumbled the key, dropping it into the milk jug. That made a lot more sense.

Tess was far too short to even think about reaching the shelf. Rodney, on the other hand, could have managed it. Rodney, who hated Brian Sutcliffe and would protect his daughter at any cost.

Seated on the white wicker couch in her conservatory, Elizabeth gave the matter some intense thought. Could she be mistaken about Rodney, after all? She kept hearing Daphne's shocked tones when she'd heard the news. *My God, Rodney. What have you done?*

He had denied it, of course. But his denials, like his concern about his daughter's possible guilt, could have been fabricated for her benefit. She would have to talk to him again. Though she could hardly accuse him of murder without some kind of proof or justification.

Sighing, she withdrew the paper she'd tucked into her pocket earlier and studied it. Neville Carbunkle had mentioned he'd seen Dickie Muggins in the kitchen arguing with Brian. She was anxious to talk to the photographer, but it would have to wait until tomorrow. Until then, she'd hold her judgment on Rodney, in the hopes that Mr. Muggins could shed new light on the puzzle.

Glancing at the clock on the mantelpiece, she noticed with some surprise that it was long past the time when Violet usually rang the bell for supper. Violet was never late with the meals. Unless she was ill.

Concerned, Elizabeth rose to her feet and hurried to the kitchen. Her anxiety deepened when she opened the door and no smell of cooking greeted her. In fact, the kitchen was as neat and clean as Violet usually left it last thing at night.

Frowning, Elizabeth headed for the pantry, expecting to find her housekeeper rummaging about in there. Instead, she found Martin, in the act of helping himself to a large chunk of cheese.

He swung around as she entered and, upon seeing her, jumped so violently he almost dropped the plate he held. By some miracle he righted it before the cheese slid off and peered at her over the rims of his glasses.

"You startled me, madam. I thought it was Violet, coming back to spy on me."

"Now why would she do that?" Elizabeth noticed the jar of pickled onions he'd taken down from the shelf. "Where is Violet, anyway? Why isn't she cooking supper?"

"Why, indeed," Martin said mournfully. "I asked her that very question myself."

Elizabeth waited, until it became obvious Martin wasn't going to continue and she was forced to ask, "So what did she say when you asked her?"

Martin placed the butcher knife he'd used on the cheese back in it's slot on the wall. "When I asked her what, madam?"

Elizabeth reminded herself that Martin was very old, somewhat senile, and one had to use infinite patience when dealing with him. "What did Violet say when you asked her why she isn't cooking supper?"

Martin thought about it. "Oh, yes. Now I remember. She said we were to eat the leftover stew." He pointed to a large pot on the shelf. "I looked at it, but it's cold. I decided I would prefer my ration of cheese and pickled onions. With buttered bread, of course."

"We don't have butter," Elizabeth reminded him. "Only margarine."

"Then I shall endeavor to do without. That dratted stuff tastes like axle grease."

Elizabeth was inclined to agree with him. "Is Violet ill? Did she say she was going to bed?"

"No, madam." Martin picked up the jar of pickled onions and tucked it under his arm. "She said she was going out. She asked me to serve the stew to the Winterhalters, which I did."

Elizabeth raised her eyebrows. In all the

years she had known Violet, and that had been all her life, she had never known the housekeeper to go out on a Sunday night. Especially when they had guests in the house. In fact, Violet rarely went out at night at all, unless it was a special event, such as the wedding. "Did she say where she was going? Is she walking?"

"No, madam. She went off in one of those infernal contraptions that make all that blasted noise and belch evil-smelling smoke everywhere, poisoning the very air we breathe."

"Do you mean a Jeep?" For the life of her, Elizabeth couldn't imagine Violet riding in a Jeep.

"No, madam. I mean a motor car."

Thoroughly mystified now, Elizabeth followed Martin out into the kitchen. "Who was driving it?"

"I'm afraid I can't answer that, madam. I couldn't see his face." Martin placed his cheese and pickled onions on the table, then opened the bread bin and took out a small loaf of bread. "Would you care to join me, madam?"

Elizabeth eyed the bread and cheese. "I don't think so, Martin. But please, don't let my presence prevent you from enjoying your supper."

"Very well, madam. But since you won't be joining me, if I may, I should like to enjoy it in my own room."

"Of course you may, Martin."

"Thank you, madam."

She watched him shuffle out the door, not without some difficulty since he was carrying the bread under one arm, the pickled onions under the other, and the plate of cheese balanced in between. She knew better than to offer her help, however. Martin became rather testy if there was the slightest hint he could not manage his own affairs.

She watched the door close behind him, her thoughts going back to Violet. She had not the slightest idea where her housekeeper might have gone. She could only hope that Violet was not in some kind of trouble. If so, there was nothing Elizabeth could do about it but wait for her housekeeper to return.

Chapter 7

"Come on, ladies. Get a bloody move on!" Rita stood in the middle of the coast road and waved her arms at the straggly bunch of women trudging far behind her. "It'll be dark soon and we have to be positioned on the cliffs by then."

"I know where I'd like to bloomin' position her," Marge muttered.

Tramping alongside her, Nellie giggled. "Leave her alone. She's in her glory when she can boss us around like this."

Marge grunted. "It's all a waste of time, if you ask me. We've been waiting five years for the Germans to invade. They're not going to come now, are they. We're winning the war. Mr. Churchill said so, and he should know."

"We haven't won it yet," Nellie said, puffing a little with the exertion of marching uphill. "We've got to invade the Nazis now and turn the tables on them."

"Well, they've been talking about that for weeks, too. Makes you wonder if this war is ever going to end."

"Shut up talking down there!" Rita

yelled, still prancing about in the middle of the road. "You want the enemy to hear you? This is supposed to be a secret mission!"

Nellie giggled again. "What makes her think they wouldn't hear her? Not much secret about that yell, is there."

"I'd like to see what she'd do if the Germans did invade," Marge mumbled. "One glimpse of a U-boat and she'd wet her knickers. She'd be off faster than a scalded cat, leaving us all to face the buggers by ourselves."

"Well, I don't think we have to worry about it. Like you said, the Nazis are not coming anywhere near this beach. Even if they did, they wouldn't get past the mines without everyone knowing about it."

"Try telling *her* that." Marge nodded at Rita, who was now marching toward them.

A faint buzz in the distance heralded a vehicle coming along the coast road at a fast pace. Rita seemed to pay no attention to it, her focus squarely on the unruly members of the Housewives League. If there was one thing Rita couldn't stand, it was being ignored.

Marge braced herself for one of Rita's explosive tirades, which more often than not were directed at her. She couldn't help it if she liked to talk. It wasn't her fault if someone talked back with her. Yet she always got the blame for what Rita liked to call a "disruption."

The roar of the engine grew louder, and Marge could tell it was a Jeep. Rita must have heard it, too. Although her back was toward the oncoming vehicle, she'd moved over to the right side of the road.

Knowing the Yanks' tendency to drive on the wrong side of the road, the group of women made sure to stand well clear of the grass verge, crowding up to the railings that lined the cliffs. They all watched with gleeful expectation as Rita stood in the road, her hands dug into her hips, and cast a baleful eye on her wayward members.

"How many times do I have to tell you," she began, "that when we're on a mission . . ."

The Jeep roared into view, plunged past Rita with room to spare and continued on its way, rocketing from side to side as it careened around the bend.

"Lucky they weren't driving on the wrong side," Marge commented. "You'd be flat as a pancake by now."

She nudged Nellie in the side as Rita glared at her, but Nellie was staring after the Jeep, her face creased in a frown. "They weren't Yanks," she said. "What were civvies doing in an American Jeep?"

"How'd you know they weren't Yanks?" Marge demanded. "They could've just been dressed up in ordinary clothes."

"Nah." Nellie looked smug. "I can tell a Yank a mile off."

"I don't know how you could tell that. I couldn't even see their faces. They had them covered with scarves."

Florrie let out a shriek that startled them all. "*Oh, my God!* It was the three musketeers!"

A chorus of horrified exclamations greeted this alarming statement.

Rita bellowed above the din. "For heaven's sake, shut up that bloody noise!"

The chatter died away, with one last echo of a whimper from Florrie.

"What are we going to do?" Nellie demanded. "They stole a flipping Jeep."

"We don't know that for sure," Rita said, assuming command once more. "We only surmise that. We can't go around accusing innocent people without being sure."

"Well, it weren't no Yanks in there, that's for sure," Nellie insisted.

"Perhaps not, but in any case, they are too far away for us to do anything about it now. I'll have a word with P.C. Dalrymple tomorrow. But for now, can we please

135

maintain silence while we assume our position on the cliffs."

Marge sighed. For a moment there it looked as if they might get out of the invasion watch for once. She might have known Rita wouldn't give up on it. It made her feel important. Rita liked to feel important. If it were up to her, she'd have the whole blinking village turn out for her missions, as she called them. Luckily for them, most of the villagers had more sense than to listen to her.

Marge joined the others as they resumed their march to the high point of the cliffs. She often wondered why she bothered to go along with it. All the plodding around trailing after Rita, watching for Germans and looking for spies. Not once had they ever caught anyone. Not once. Not even when they had a German pilot cornered in the windmill. There was always someone else there to seize the glory.

She could almost feel sorry for Rita, if she didn't know the woman enjoyed every minute of it. Pity her when the war was over. Rita Crumm would have to find another way to throw her weight around. Wonder what she'd do. Probably get rid of Lady Elizabeth and take over the Manor House if she had her way.

Marge pulled a face, imagining what life would be like in Sitting Marsh with Rita Crumm as lady of the manor. She'd blinking move, she would. Go and live in North Horsham.

"You got a blister or something?"

Marge jumped as Nellie hissed in her ear. "No, why?"

"You had a sour look on your face." Nellie grinned. "You need to piddle?"

Marge scowled at her. "No, I don't. I don't know —" She broke off, her breath catching in her throat. They had just rounded the bend, and Rita stood transfixed in front of them, looking at something straight ahead. The way she stood there, all still and quiet, gave Marge the chills.

"What's she looking at?" Nellie whispered loudly.

The rest of the group had halted, all apparently struck by Rita's odd posture. They huddled together, afraid to speak, and Marge was quite certain that the dreaded invasion had begun after all.

Then Rita turned and came back to them at a run. "You were right, Florrie," she said, sounding breathless. "Three men, all with scarves tied over their faces."

"Oh, my," Florrie moaned.

The other women started muttering, until Rita silenced them with a sharp raise of her hand. "This is our chance," she said, her voice low and hoarse with excitement. "We're going to capture the three musketeers."

"How the bloody hell do you think we're going to do that?" Nellie demanded.

"Shhh!" Rita put a finger over her lips. "We want to take them by surprise."

"And they're going to come along quietly? I don't think so." Nellie crossed her arms. "The best thing we can do is get George and Sid up here. They've got the authority."

"I've got authority, too," Rita said stiffly. "As General of the Housewives League, I have the authority to apprehend anyone endangering the lives of the villagers."

Nellie smirked. "Says who?"

"Says everyone. That's who. It's understood."

"So how are they endangering us?"

"They could shove the Jeep over the cliffs and it could hit a mine and blow all our heads off."

Shocked cries arose among the group. "Ere, I'm orf," someone said.

"Me, too." There was a general movement of the crowd to turn tail.

"No one is going anywhere," Rita muttered fiercely. "They've been trying to cath these criminals for months. All that damage they've done to the American vehicles and property — we can't let them go now."

"Even if we do catch them, how are we going to get them back to the village?" Florrie ventured.

Rita quelled her with a glare. "All right, what we have to do is keep them talking while someone goes down to the village for George and Sid."

Nellie sniggered. "How do you think you're going to keep them talking? Chat about the weather?"

"I'm not going to," Rita said calmly. "You are."

Nellie's grin vanished. "Me? Not on your life."

"You have to do it." Rita put on her stubborn look. "You're the youngest, and not bad looking. You're the only one they'll take any notice of; and after all, you've had plenty of experience chatting up the boys."

Nellie looked offended. "Here, what does that mean?"

"I only meant that you're the most experienced one to do this. Think what it will mean, to be the one who catches the three musketeers. Some of the most wanted criminals in the country."

Nellie stared at her, and Marge could tell that she was weighing the price of glory against the need for self-preservation. Finally, she said, "All right, I'll do it. But you'd better all be close behind me. And someone had better get down to the village really fast because I don't know how long I can keep them talking."

Rita beamed. "Good for you, Nellie. You won't regret this, I promise you."

It wasn't often Nellie got praise from Rita. If ever. She turned red and muttered, "I bloody hope not."

Rita turned to Florrie. "You go down to the village, Florrie, and fetch George and Sid. If they're not together, then send them up here one at a time. And make it fast. We don't want to lose them now we've got them in our grasp."

Florrie had been turning even more pale throughout this speech. Finally she spluttered, "Oh, I couldn't. Really I couldn't."

"Of course you can," Rita said, losing all vestige of patience. "All you've got to do is run down the hill and tell George the three musketeers are up here and to come right away. It's downhill all the way. How hard is that?"

"Why can't Marge go?" Florrie whined.

Rita uttered a grunt of contempt. "Look at her. She's twice your size. It would take her forever to get down there. You can do it in half the time."

Marge was about to protest, then thought better of it. After all, she didn't want to be the one to go down to the village. She wanted to stay and watch the excitement.

At last, Florrie was persuaded, and she set off at a panicky run in the direction of the village.

"Now," Rita said, giving Nellie a pat on the shoulder. "Off you go. Tell them you're on your way home and ask them for a lift or something. Or pretend you've lost your dog and want them to help you look for it."

"I haven't got a dog," Nellie said, beginning to look scared.

"I know that." Rita actually grinned, though her mouth looked as if it were fighting it. "But they don't know that, do they. Just get on with it. We have to stop them before they leave and disappear again."

Nellie looked really worried now, and Marge felt sorry for her. "Maybe I should go with her," she said, wondering what on earth had made her say that.

"No, it's better if she goes alone. That way they won't feel threatened."

"Maybe they won't, but I flipping will." Nellie looked around the group. "You'll all come running if I yell for help, won't you?"

Everyone nodded, though no one looked as if they really meant it.

With a sick feeling in her stomach, Marge watched Nellie walk slowly up the road. They were sending her into danger, all alone, straight into the arms of the most wanted criminals in the country. What on earth were they thinking?

Faced with the prospect of eating left-over stew, Elizabeth decided instead to take a ride down to the Tudor Arms and buy two of Alfie's delicious Cornish pasties. Just the thought of them made her feel hungry, and she wasted no time in getting her motorcycle out from the stables.

It was still early enough that the pub wouldn't be too crowded, and with any luck she could slip in and out without attracting too much attention. It would do her good to get out of the house, she told herself as she swept down the hill. Too much time spent alone allowed her to dwell on Earl and what horrors he might be facing.

News of the bombing raids on Germany were prevalent on the wireless these days. One could hardly turn it on without hearing about the planes lost and the courageous men who didn't return. She seldom listened to the news now, and only turned on the wireless when one of her favorite programs was on.

One could hardly dig one's head into the sand, however. What with the wireless reports, the newspaper, and talk on everyone's lips, it was difficult to escape the rumors about an imminent invasion of Europe by the Allies. Just the mere mention of it was enough to turn her stomach and fill her heart with fear.

Turning into the parking lot, she was thankful to see no Jeeps parked there. A couple of bicycles leaned against the fence, but other than that it seemed the evening's festivities were yet to begin. Of course, with Priscilla on her honeymoon, the Sunday talent concert would not be held. Then again, most of the locals walked to the pub and could already be inside enjoying their evening pint.

Although aware that the rules of etiquette had been relaxed considerably since the outbreak of the war, Elizabeth still felt uncomfortable entering the pub unescorted.

Still, the thought of those Cornish pasties called to her, and she couldn't ignore the hunger pangs. She headed for the door, her mouth watering.

The familiar smell of beer, tobacco, and the musty odor of the heavy oak beams was as potent as ever. The level of chatter lowered considerably as she made her way to the bar. Several tables were occupied in the saloon bar, and recognizing the locals, she acknowledged them all with a gracious wave of her hand.

The gentlemen rose, until she waved them back into their seats. "I shan't be long," she told them. "Please sit down and enjoy your evening."

Alfie, the ruddy-faced jovial barman, greeted her with a smile. "Come for your usual drop of sherry, your ladyship? Sit right down and I'll pour you one."

"Actually I came for Cornish pasties." Elizabeth glanced hungrily at the display case on the counter. "I won't be stopping for a drink tonight."

"Got a nice bottle of cream sherry just come in." Alfie reached under the counter, brought out a bottle, and waved it at her. "Shame to waste it on those what don't appreciate a good sherry when they see one."

Elizabeth hesitated. The house *was* awfully lonely without Violet there. Thinking about her missing housekeeper got her worried again. She climbed up on a stool and said demurely, "Just one, then, Alfie. Thank you."

"My pleasure, m'm." Alfie poured the brown liquid into a glass and pushed it toward her.

She could smell the sweet, tangy aroma of it even before she lifted the glass to her lips. The first sip burned her throat, as it always did, and she put down the drink. "I don't suppose you've seen Violet in the last hour or two?"

Alfie seemed surprised. "Violet? In here? I don't think she's ever set foot in this pub. Not as long as I've been here, anyhow."

"Well, she doesn't usually go off somewhere without telling me, either." Elizabeth glanced around the room in the faint hope of seeing her housekeeper's bony features.

"Maybe she took a walk. It's a nice night."

Elizabeth shook her head. "Martin said she went off in a motorcar. I wasn't aware that Violet knew anyone who had a motorcar."

Alfie looked sympathetic. "I know you must be worried about her. Finding that Sutcliffe chap dead at the wedding yesterday puts everyone on edge. Nasty business, that."

"Yes, it was."

"Can't say I'm all that surprised, though. Smarmy blighter he was, though one shouldn't speak ill of the dead."

"Oh, that's right. He had a room here, didn't he." Forgetting Violet for the moment, Elizabeth seized the opportunity to pursue her investigation. "I take it you didn't care for the gentleman."

Alfie snorted. "That weren't no gentleman. Troublemaker, that's what he was. Almost came to a punch-up the other night. I had to step in and calm things down."

"Oh, dear." Elizabeth wrinkled her brow. "What happened?"

Alfie nodded at the customer who had come up to the bar unnoticed by Elizabeth. "Ask Dave here. He knows better than I do."

Elizabeth turned to the newcomer, who touched his forehead with his fingers.

"Evening, your ladyship."

"Oh, yes. Mr. Murphy, isn't it? You own a fishing boat, I believe."

The young man nodded. "Yes, m'm. The Murphys have been fishing the North Sea ever since we came over from Ireland."

"Yes, I knew your father." Elizabeth

studied the pleasant face. "So you were here when the argument began?"

"Yes, m'm." Dave Murphy hesitated, and glanced at Alfie.

"It's all right, Dave." Alfie grabbed a tankard from above his head and stuck it under one of the pumps. "You can say anything to her ladyship. She's heard it all before."

Dave coughed, his cheeks growing warm. "Well, this chap Sutcliffe, he was poking fun at one of the customers."

"Dickie, the photographer," Alfie explained.

Elizabeth raised her eyebrows. "Really. I wasn't aware that Mr. Sutcliffe and Mr. Muggins knew each other before the day of the wedding."

"I don't think they did know each other," Dave said, looking even more uncomfortable. "Not before that night, anyhow. They both were staying here, for the wedding."

"That's right," Alfie put in. "Dickie was down from North Horsham and was taking photographs the night before the wedding. He didn't want to drag all his stuff back home and then have to bring it all down again the next day. So he asked if he could leave it here. I suggested he stay the night, so he did."

"I see." Elizabeth turned back to Dave. "Brian Sutcliffe was making fun of him? In what way?"

Dave loudly cleared his throat. "Well, Dickie is a bit, you know . . ." He looked at Alfie for help.

"He's a poof," Alfie said.

Puzzled, Elizabeth turned to him. "I beg your pardon?"

Dave coughed again, louder than necessary. "I don't think —"

Alfie ignored him. "You know. A fruit."

Elizabeth stared at him blankly.

Alfie flapped his fingers at her. "A queer, your ladyship."

"Alfie, I really don't think —" Dave began, but much to Elizabeth's amazement, Alfie interrupted him, his voice rising to a remarkable high falsetto.

"You are just too, too precious, dahling," he squeaked, and flapped his fingers in her face again.

Slowly, realization dawned. "Oh," she said faintly. "Now I understand." She'd heard of such people, of course. One could hardly live in London as long as she had and not be aware of all its diversities. "And Brian found out, I suppose."

"You can hardly miss it," Alfie said.

"Anyway," Dave said hurriedly, "Sutcliffe

was making some off-color remarks, saying things like Dickie would look lovely in a wedding dress, and . . . well, things like that. Dickie finally lost his temper and threw his beer all over him. Then Sutcliffe got nasty and said he was going to write to the North Horsham newspaper and tell everyone he was a . . . well, you know."

"Ruin his career, that would," Alfie muttered. "I mean, most people just think he's a bit off, you know. But you put that kind of thing in the newspaper for everyone to read, well, no one would hire him to take photographs at weddings anymore. Or anything else for that matter. Wouldn't look right, would it."

"Indeed it wouldn't. What happened, then?"

Dave took up the story again. "Well, that was the strange part. Dickie stood up to him. Sounded a lot different, he did. Warned Sutcliffe to leave him alone or he'd find himself in some bad trouble. Then he asked Alfie for his key and left."

"That's right," Alfie said. "He went up to his room."

Having heard enough for the present, Elizabeth changed the subject. She finished her sherry, bought her Cornish pasties, and left, eager now to talk to the fussy photographer again. Especially since it seemed he had a very good reason to thoroughly dislike the late Brian Sutcliffe.

Chapter 8

Marge stood with the others and watched Nellie walk slowly up the road and disappear around the curve. Rita beckoned with an imperious wave of her hand and they set off after her. When they got quite a bit closer, Rita flapped her hand in a command for them to stop, and they halted, obeying Rita's signal to remain silent.

Rita crept forward, bent double at the waist, using the bushes on the grass verge to shield her. One by one, the rest of the housewives crept forward. Marge was the third to go, and she had a lot of trouble bending down low enough to be hidden as she crept toward her bush.

They were too far away to hear anything, but Marge had a pretty good view of what was going on. She could see Nellie pointing down the road away from the women, saying something that made the three men turn to look in that direction.

They stood close to the edge of the cliffs, and the Jeep's front wheels rested on top of the barbed wire that ran along the other side of the railings. It did look as if they were trying to push the Jeep over the cliffs, where it would crash to the beach below.

Marge felt a shiver go all the way down her back. Didn't they realize there were mines hidden in the sand? No one knew where they were. If one went off when Nellie was standing that close to the edge she could get really hurt. Even killed. Marge felt sick again. They should never have let her go up there. Stupid, stupid, stupid.

Nellie had turned back to the men now and seemed to be arguing with them. Marge heard Rita mutter something, and then everything happened at once.

Marge could hardly believe her eyes when she saw Nellie reach out and grab the scarf from one of the men's faces. Rita rose to her feet, but before she had time to gather breath to yell, the man grabbed hold of Nellie while the other two dragged the Jeep back onto the road.

"Come on," Rita roared, "after them!"

"Oh, poop," Marge muttered, and scrambled to her feet.

Rita galloped toward Nellie, screeching at the top of her lungs. Several of the women followed her, but more at a fast walk than a trot. Marge struggled valiantly to keep up, and even managed to pass a couple of the slower members.

It was all a wasted effort, after all. Rita was within a few feet when Nellie was thrust into the back of the Jeep, all three men jumped in at once, and the vehicle bounced off across the grass and onto the coast road. By the time the rest of them caught up with Rita, Nellie and her captors had disappeared.

"All right, what do I put next?" Sadie stuck the end of the pen in her mouth and stared down at her untidy scrawl. "He's never going to be able to read this mess."

"He will if you write slower." Polly bounced up and down on her bed. "You're scribbling that as if the end of the world is coming."

Leaning her elbows on Polly's dressing table, Sadie sighed. "I'm not used to writing letters. I don't write much at all, really. Once I got out of school I never bothered with it."

"Well, you should, or you'll forget how to do it." She held out her hand. "Let me read it."

Reluctantly, Sadie handed it over.

Polly scanned the few lines, a frown marring her face. "'Dear soldier,'" she read out. "'My name is Sadie Buttons and I work as a housemaid at the Manor

153

House'" She looked up. "Is that all you wrote so far?"

Sadie shrugged. "I don't know what to put."

Polly shook her head and handed the letter back. "All right, start by telling him what you like."

"I can't put that in a letter!"

"Not that, silly." Polly reached across the bed to push a hand under her pillow. "Here, read this. It's from Marlene and she says what the soldiers want to hear."

Sadie took the crumpled pages from her and read through them. "They want to know what my life is like and what's going on in the village?"

"Yeah, ordinary sort of stuff. It's what they miss most, Marlene says. Just the everyday goings on."

"Sounds boring." Sadie scowled. "Nothing exciting ever happens in Sitting Marsh."

Polly gasped. "How can you say that, Sadie Buttons! Just yesterday a bloke got himself killed at a wedding."

"I can't tell a stranger that! He'd think we lived in a den of iniquity."

"What does that mean?"

"I dunno, but it sounds evil."

"Well, then, tell him about the summer fete, and about going to the pictures in

North Horsham, and who your favorite film stars are, and what music you like, and your favorite song —"

"All right, all right," Sadie muttered, scribbling like mad. "That's enough to fill two letters."

"Put something personal in it, too. They like that."

Sadie dipped her pen in the inkwell, shook it, then paused. "Wonder if they'll put Tess in prison for killing her boyfriend."

"We don't know if she did kill him yet." Polly slid off the bed. "Like you said, it could've been an accident."

"Well, I tell you one thing, her mother will be happy he's dead."

Polly gasped. "That's an awful thing to say! No one should be happy he's dead."

"Well, at least she'll be happy he won't be marrying Tess. I heard her tell Tess that she never thought a daughter of hers would stoop so low as to associate with such filthy scum."

Polly's jaw dropped. "She said that? I didn't think posh people talked like that."

Sadie grinned. "You don't know the half of it. I worked for a posh family in London for a while, and you wouldn't believe half of what was going on there."

Polly bounced back onto the bed. "Go on, tell me!"

Sadie shook her head. "Nah, I'll tell you another time. I've got to get back to the manor before it gets too dark. I can't see without me lights and it's really creepy riding up the driveway in the pitch black."

"Can't you see in the moonlight?"

"I can when there's a moon." Sadie capped the pen, folded her letter, and got up from the chair. "There ain't no moon tonight, though. Not for another three nights, anyway."

Polly looked impressed. "How'd you know that?"

"I got a calendar, haven't I." Sadie handed her the letter. "Thanks for helping me with that."

"I wasn't much help." Polly slid off the bed and picked up her own letter from the dressing table. She slipped Sadie's letter inside and sealed it up. "There. I'll post it tomorrow on me way up to the manor."

"All right." Sadie moved to the door. "How long do you think it will be before we get an answer?"

"Don't know. I s'pose it depends on how quick it gets across the ocean."

"It don't seem right, does it. Those men so far away from home, and nobody bothers to even write them a letter."

"Well, they've got lots from the village now. Marlene said they were real excited to get them, too."

"Yeah." Sadie smiled with pride. "We did a good thing, Polly."

"Yes, we did." Polly got up and hugged her friend. "Be careful riding home."

Calling out to Polly's ma, Sadie let herself out the front door and climbed on her bicycle. Already the night had crept in from the ocean, leaving just a pale pink glow above the dense woods. Sadie could see the silhouette of the old windmill as she cycled up the hill, and above it a formation of airplanes heading for the base. The rumble of their engines floated down as they circled inland and then faded into the shadows of the evening sky.

A moment later Sadie heard the roar of another engine. She looked up, expecting to see a straggler in the sky. No one liked to see that. It usually meant that something was wrong with the plane, and the pilot was having trouble getting home.

The sky appeared to be empty, and she realized that what she'd heard was the sound of a Jeep's engine. She peered ahead in the shadowy twilight, watching for it to come around the bend. The Yanks never could remember which side of the road to drive on.

When she eventually caught sight of the Jeep, it wasn't on the road at all. It was bouncing across the downs, heading for the woods. It was hard to see in the gathering darkness, but it looked like there were four people sitting in it.

Frowning, Sadie pedaled on. What would the Yanks be doing taking a Jeep into the woods? They had to be doing some training. "Maneuvers" they called it. She heard them now and again, when the wind was in the right direction. The soft explosions in the distance and bright flashes of light had scared the dickens out of the villagers until they got used to them.

Smiling to herself, she put her head down and pumped faster. It would soon be too dark to see, and she still had that driveway waiting for her.

Violet still wasn't home when Elizabeth arrived back at the manor, and, more worried than ever, she made herself a cup of tea and sat down at the kitchen table to eat her Cornish pasties. They didn't taste quite as good as she remembered, though she was generous enough to allow that her anxiety had probably tainted her appetite.

Rather than sit in absolute silence, she switched on the wireless and listened to the gentle strains of a Brahms symphony. She was halfway through her second pasty when the announcer's voice declared solemnly, "This is British Broadcasting, and here is the news. The Allies bombed areas of France again this evening, inflicting heavy damage. Casualties are light, and the War Office reports —"

Elizabeth lunged for the radio and switched it off. The dogs, who had been sleeping under the table, leapt to their feet, growls rumbling in their throats.

"It's all right, darlings." Elizabeth dropped to her knees and patted both their heads. "It's quite all right."

But it wasn't all right. She had seen no Jeeps in the courtyard when she'd put her motorcycle away. None at all. And there had been none at the pub. What was it Earl had said? *Things are heating up.* They were getting ready for something. Something big. No one would know about it until after it was underway. And then it would be too late.

Her fear became overwhelming, and she clasped both dogs to her, burying her face in their soft fur. She prayed as she'd never prayed before. She was still on her knees when the shrill jangle of the telephone shattered the silence.

Nellie winced as the Jeep bounced over roots and in and out of deep ruts between the trees. The jolts jarred her teeth and rattled her bones until she thought they must all be broken. What frightened her most was that the driver of the Jeep couldn't possibly see in the dark, and she expected any minute to crash into a tree and be struck dead. It was somewhat of a relief when they burst out from the trees and swung into a narrow lane bordered by hedges too tall to see over, even in daylight.

"Where are you taking me?" she demanded, struggling to free herself from the rope that bound her hands.

"You'll see," muttered the driver.

She stared at her kidnappers, still numb with disbelief. Not only had she let herself be captured and tied up like a trussed chicken, the "men" had turned out to be young kids, probably still at school. After she'd dragged the scarf from one of their faces, the other two had uncovered theirs as well.

What a fool she was going to look, being kidnapped by schoolboys. "You're going to

160

be in dead trouble when they catch you," she said, glaring at the boy seated next to her.

He shrugged. "So who's going to catch us? That bunch of old biddies squealing like stuck pigs back there?"

"The American MPs, that's who." She smiled with grim satisfaction. "Just wait until they get hold of you. The Yanks can be really nasty when they get fired up. I've seen them in action."

"I just bet you have," the boy sneered, making her itch to slap his face.

"Shut up, Robbie," the driver snapped. "Just ignore her. You'll give too much away if you talk to her."

"Robbie?" Nellie nodded. "Nice name that. Robbie who?"

The driver flung a vicious scowl at Robbie. "Now look what you've bleeding done. Now she knows your name, stupid."

"Yeah, well who was stupid enough to let her pull his scarf off then? Bighead Stan, that's who."

"Robbie and Stan." Nellie was fast losing her fear. In fact, she was beginning to enjoy herself. "Now we only have one name to go." She looked at the boy seated next to Stan. "So what's your name, love?"

The third boy didn't answer her, and her

apprehension returned as the Jeep swung off the road and came to a halt in front of a gate.

"Open it," Stan ordered.

Neither of his companions moved.

"Open the bloody gate, Robbie," Stan yelled.

"Why me? Why can't Jimmy do it?"

Both boys turned around to glare at him. "If you can't keep your bloody big mouth shut I'll shut it for you," Stan muttered. "Now get out and open the bloody gate."

"All right, keep your hair on. I'm going." Robbie climbed out and shoved the gate open. He waited until Stan had driven the Jeep into the field, then closed the gate behind it.

Nellie considered making a run for it, but with her hands tied behind her back she'd never make it. Better to wait until she could free herself and then escape. Her uneasiness increased as the Jeep bumped across the plowed ruts. It was pitch dark now, but she could see the outline of a huge barn in front of them.

They halted when they reached it, and this time Robbie jumped out without being asked. After dragging the huge doors open, he stood back and Stan drove the Jeep inside. Nellie's spirits dropped as the doors squeaked shut behind her. The barn smelled of manure and dried hay, and the dust tickled her nose, making her sneeze.

A beam of light probed the darkness from a torch in Stan's hand. He cut the engine and jumped out. "Bring her over here," he ordered, pointing to a ladder leading up to a high ledge.

Despite her struggles, Nellie was helpless as the two boys grasped her arms and forced her over to the ladder. She was beginning to realize now that though they were much younger than her, she was powerless against them together. Once more her fear was thick in her throat.

Her hands were roughly set free, then Stan ordered, "Get up there!" and gave her a shove.

"Keep your filthy hands off me," she snarled, managing to sound threatening in spite of the heavy hammering of her heart.

"Or you'll what?" Stan said nastily.

"You'll find out." She decided to do what she was told for now. Until she could work out a way to escape from these three thugs. Then she'd see they got what they deserved. Scrambling up the ladder, she prayed they weren't staring up her skirt.

Safely on the ledge, she was surprised to see a blanket laid out on the floor of the small loft. An oil lamp sat a few feet away with a box of matches in the saucer. The newspaper crumpled up on the edge of the blanket smelled of fish. Apparently her kidnappers had bought supper from the fish and chip shop in the High Street.

Nellie knew the owners, Ethel and Reg Clements. Once it was reported she was missing, maybe Ethel would remember she'd served three strangers and give George and Sid some idea where to start looking. By now Rita and the others must have told the constables what had happened.

To her immense relief, none of the boys climbed up after her. Instead, they dragged the ladder away from the ledge, so she had no way to get down, then left her in semi-darkness while they huddled below and started discussing what they were going to do next.

"We can't leave her here all night," Robbie said, his voice rising almost to a whine. "What are we going to do?"

"Shut up," Stan ordered. "Let me think."

"Where are we going to sleep if she's up there?" Jimmy demanded.

"We're not going to sleep. We've got work to do. We can sleep when we get back. Down here. There's plenty of straw to sleep on."

"Well, I'm going to get the blanket," Robbie said, whining again. "The straw scratches me arms too much to sleep."

"Too bad. You'll have to put up with it tonight."

"Why can't she sleep down here?"

" 'Cos she might be able to escape, stupid. If she's stuck up there, there's no way she can get past us."

"I told you this was a lousy idea," Robbie said, beginning to sound panicky. "I wish I'd never listened to you. I might have known something would go wrong. I think we should just go home and forget about the whole thing."

"Not on your life!"

"Not bloody likely!"

The other two boys had spoken at once. Robbie started to say something else, then obviously thought better of it.

"Now," Stan said, "we've got to take the Jeep back to the cliffs and push her over. Just like we planned. That way everyone will think it's the three musketeers what did the rest of it. They'll never think of looking for anyone else."

"Until *she* tells them," Jimmy said.

An ominous silence followed, while

Nellie sat above them, holding her breath. Then Stan said brusquely, "We'll worry about her when we've finished what we came to do. Now let's get on with it."

The scuffling sounds told Nellie they were climbing back into the Jeep. Then the doors were dragged open, the Jeep roared to life and the light flashed off, leaving her in total darkness. Moments later she heard the doors close again, and the sound of the Jeep's engine gradually faded into silence.

She was alone. Her and the rats. It was not a pleasant thought.

Chapter 9

Elizabeth stared at the telephone, willing it to stop ringing. She didn't want to answer it. If it was bad news, she didn't want to hear it. Why else would someone be ringing this late?

When the double ring sounded for the fourth time she could stand it no longer, and she rose to her feet. The jangle cut off abruptly as she lifted the receiver from the hook.

George's voice answered her, striking terror in her heart. "Is it Violet?" she asked breathlessly. "Has something happened to her?"

George sounded surprised when he answered. "Violet? What makes you think it's Violet? Isn't she there?"

Elizabeth slowly let out her breath. It couldn't be about Earl. If something had happened to him, she wouldn't know until someone from the base rang her. "Don't tell me there's been another murder," she said, praying that wasn't it.

"No, m'm. At least not yet."

George's enigmatic answer did nothing

to relieve her mind. "What's happened, George?"

"It's Nellie Smith, m'm. I thought you'd like to know. She's been kidnapped."

"Kidnapped?" Elizabeth stared incredulously at the wall in front of her. "Who on earth would want to kidnap Nellie? She doesn't have any family, and no money to speak off. At least as far as I'm aware —"

"It were the three musketeers, m'm. Apparently they were up to their tricks again, and Nellie went to keep them talking while Florrie came to get me, but by the time we got up there they was gone and so was Nellie."

"Nellie confronted the three musketeers? By *herself*? What was she thinking?"

"Well, it seems that Rita Crumm's bunch were with her, but standing a ways back. Nellie pulled one of the men's scarf off and got a look at his face, so I reckon they took off with her so she couldn't identify the culprits."

Elizabeth groaned. "Do you have any idea where she might be? Have they asked for a ransom?"

"Haven't heard a peep out of 'em, m'm."

"Then we'll have to organize a search for her."

"Yes, m'm. That's what I thought."

"I'll get my motorcycle and be right down." Elizabeth was about to replace the telephone when George's urgent voice stayed her hand.

"No, your ladyship. Not tonight. Without lights it would be like looking for a needle in a haystack. We'll have to wait for first light tomorrow."

"She could well be dead by then."

"I'm sorry, m'm. There's not much else I can do. It ain't safe for people to be tramping about in the dark."

"It isn't safe for Nellie to be in the clutches of those criminals, either, George."

"I know that, m'm. But I can't be responsible for sending unauthorized persons into danger. It's more than I dare do."

Elizabeth sighed. He was right. They would have to wait for morning and pray they weren't too late. Another thought occurred to her, and once more the feeling of panic almost overwhelmed her. "George, Violet seems to have disappeared as well. You don't think that has anything to do with Nellie's kidnapping, do you?"

George sounded wary when he answered. "I really couldn't say, m'm. I wouldn't think so, but if she doesn't turn up by the morning give me a ring and we'll add her to the missing list."

Elizabeth didn't often cry, but right then she could have sat down and bawled. There just seemed no end to their troubles lately. If only Earl were there to reassure her. Under the circumstances, the chances of that were extremely unlikely.

She replaced the telephone and at the same moment heard the sound of a key in the back door. It opened, and Violet appeared in the doorway, her face flushed, wearing a print frock that Elizabeth couldn't remember seeing before. Without giving her housekeeper a chance to open her mouth, Elizabeth demanded, "Where on earth have you been? Why didn't you let me know you were going out? Do you have any idea how worried I've been about you? This really is most inconsiderate of you, Violet, and not like you at all."

The glow in Violet's cheeks burned even more. Pursing her lips, she placed her handbag on the kitchen table before saying crisply, "I told that old fool to tell you I was going out. I suppose he forgot. I should have left a note."

Somewhat mollified, Elizabeth did her best to curb her temper. Her fright, followed by her relief that Violet was not in the hands of some cutthroats, had materialized in a fit of anger, and she had no right to be angry at Violet for taking a night off duty.

"He told me you were going out," she admitted, slumping onto a chair. "He just didn't tell me where."

"That's because I didn't tell him where I was going." Violet peered more closely at her. "I'm sorry I worried you, Lizzie. I didn't mean to frighten you. You might know I wouldn't be anywhere where I could come to harm."

Elizabeth passed a hand across her eyes. "No, you're right. It's just . . ." To her horror she heard her voice break and quickly took a deep breath.

Violet shrugged off the cardigan she wore and went into the pantry. She came out carrying a bottle of brandy in one hand and a glass in the other. "Here," she said, pouring the golden liquid into the glass, "you look as if you need this right now."

For once Elizabeth didn't argue. She took the glass and cautiously sipped the drink, wincing as it burned her throat. "Nellie Smith's been kidnaped," she said, as she put the glass on the table.

Violet clutched her throat. "Oh, my. *Nellie?* Who would want to kidnap her?"

"The three musketeers, apparently." Wearily, Elizabeth recounted the story George had given her.

"And they don't have any idea where they took her?" Violet demanded, when Elizabeth finished the tale.

"No, they don't. The last thing they saw was a stolen Jeep racing down the coast road. She could be anywhere. In London now, for all we know. We'll be organizing a search in the morning, but we don't have much to go on."

Violet sat down at the table. "Sorry, Lizzie. I know how worried you must be."

"It's not only that. It's everything else. What with Brian Sutcliffe's murder and —"

"Major Monroe?"

Elizabeth avoided her gaze. "Yes, I'm worried about him, too."

Violet leaned forward and patted her hand. "I know. Cheer up, duck. He'll be back, you'll see."

"I hope so." Elizabeth made an effort to smile. "So tell me where you went and why you couldn't tell Martin."

Violet straightened her back. "I didn't tell him because I wasn't in the mood for his sarcastic remarks. I went out with Charlie Gibbons."

Elizabeth stared at her. "Wally's friend? How did that happen?"

Violet shrugged, looking more like a young girl than an elderly woman. "We got

172

on really well at the wedding and he rang me up while you were out this afternoon and asked if I'd like to go to out with him for dinner in North Horsham. He brought his car down from Newcastle. That's where he lives. So I cooked a stew for the Winterhalters and told Martin to serve them." She looked worried. "I hope he did."

As far as Elizabeth could remember, Violet had never had a serious relationship with a man. Judging from the starry-eyed look on her face, Charlie Gibbons seemed to have made a startling first impression on the contentious housekeeper. "Yes, he did," she assured the housekeeper. "I imagine you had an enjoyable evening."

"Dinner was very nice," Violet said primly.

"I'm sure it was." Elizabeth struggled to sound casual. "Are you seeing him again, or is he going back to Newcastle tomorrow?"

"No, he's staying with Neville until Wally and Priscilla get back from their honeymoon, so he can help Priscilla move into Wally's cottage. Fiona's staying in Priscilla's flat so she can help, too."

"How nice for you," Elizabeth murmured.

Violet gave her a sharp look. "You don't approve."

"It's not up to me to approve or not. It's not my business." Elizabeth wrestled with her conscience for a full second before blurting out, "I just don't want you to be hurt, that's all. I mean, he's going back to Newcastle sooner or later, isn't he?"

Violet met her gaze squarely. "Newcastle is a good deal closer than America."

Elizabeth slumped back in her chair. "Yes, I suppose it is."

Violet's hand closed over hers. "Lizzie, don't worry about me. I'm at an age when I know all the pitfalls. I'm just having a bit of fun, that's all. Don't begrudge me that."

"Oh, Violet." Elizabeth clasped the bony hand in hers. "I would never begrudge you a second of happiness. These days one has to grasp every chance one can and live for the moment. Have all the fun you want. I wish you nothing but joy."

"Thank you." Violet looked close to tears. "I wish the same for you, dear Lizzie." She got up from the table, saying brusquely, "I'm weary. I'm going to bed. I suggest you do the same."

Elizabeth fell asleep that night with a heavy heart and awoke the next morning with a sick feeling of dread that proved im-

174

possible to shake. Sadie and Polly joined them for breakfast, as did Martin, who seemed even grumpier than usual. Especially when Violet dumped a plate of porridge in front of him with a cheerful, "Eat up, you old buzzard. This'll clear you out and make you feel a lot better in no time."

Martin glared at her over his specs. "I do not require anything to *clear me out,* as you so crudely phrase it, and I'll thank you to refrain from making such personal remarks in front of the servants."

"I ain't a servant," Polly protested. "I'm Lady Elizabeth's assistant."

"And I'm her personal housemaid," Sadie put in, "so put that in your pipe and smoke it."

Martin looked at them both with distaste. "May I remind you that you are sharing a table with her ladyship, a practice I find quite deplorable I might add, and that such abominable language will not be tolerated in her ladyship's presence."

Sadie had the grace to look repentant. "Sorry, m'm." she mumbled.

"I should think so." Violet placed a bowl of porridge in front of the two girls. "Now eat up. It will give your mouths something to do other than torment Martin."

Sadie looked up in surprise. "You're in

good spirits this morning, Vi. What's up with you?"

"My name is Violet," the housekeeper answered, "and nothing's up with me. Now finish your meal."

Sadie exchanged mystified glances with Polly. Elizabeth could hardly blame her. Normally Violet would have been screeching at the top of her lungs at Sadie for her impudence.

Deciding it was time to bring a more serious topic to the table, Elizabeth said quietly, "I'm afraid I have some bad news to tell you."

Sadie and Polly stared at her with apprehension on their faces, while Martin merely looked resigned. "The Germans are invading us," he muttered. "I knew it was only a matter of time."

"No, Martin. They are not invading us. In fact, this has nothing to do with the war. At least, not directly."

"What is it, then, m'm?" Sadie sat with her spoon halfway to her mouth, the soggy oatmeal dripping from it onto her plate.

"It's Nellie Smith." Elizabeth paused, trying to find an easy way to say it, then gave up. "I'm afraid she's been kidnapped."

Shocked cries from the girls mingled

with Martin's dry comment, "By the Americans, no doubt."

Elizabeth ignored him. "Apparently she confronted the three musketeers last night on the coast road. Managed to pull the scarf from one of their faces and they took her away in the Jeep they were driving."

"They must have stolen the Jeep," Polly said. "Poor Nellie. What will happen to her?"

"I saw a Jeep last night," Sadie said, frowning. "It were making a run for it towards the woods. I thought it was the Yanks on maneuvers, but now I come to think about it, I didn't see them wearing military caps. It were dark, but I could swear they weren't wearing uniforms."

Elizabeth jumped up from the table, taking Martin by surprise. He dropped his spoon with a clatter and struggled painfully to his feet, one inch at a time.

"Are you sure?" Elizabeth hurried over to the telephone. "I should let George know at once."

"I'm sure about the Jeep," Sadie said. "But I couldn't honestly say who was in it."

Elizabeth dialed the number and waited. She counted seven rings before George finally answered. "Sadie saw the Jeep last night," she said, bypassing the usual greeting. "It was heading into the woods."

"Right, then that's where we'll start. Mrs. Crumm and her lot are here already. I'll get them off right away." His voice faded as he spoke to someone in the distance. "Beg pardon? Yes, all right." He spoke into the mouthpiece again. "Sorry, m'm. Mrs. Crumm took exception to me using the phrase 'her lot.' She said to tell you her *troops* are ready to embark on their mission."

Elizabeth almost smiled. "Tell Mrs. Crumm I am eternally grateful."

"Yes, m'm. Oh, and I heard from the inspector. He says he'll be down here in a day or two to look into the wedding guest murder."

The news gave Elizabeth a jolt. She'd been so wrapped up in Nellie's kidnapping, she had neglected her promise to the Winterhalters that she would do what she could to investigate the murder. "Thank you, George." She paused. "I will join the search party as soon as I can. I have an important errand to run first."

"That's all right, your ladyship. I don't think you should be tramping around in the woods anyway. Not fitting, is it."

"George, when one of my tenants is in trouble, doing what is fitting is the least of my concerns."

"Yes, m'm. So I've noticed."

His dry tone told Elizabeth he would rather she stayed out of the search altogether. He might know that wasn't going to happen. At least he wasn't aware of her investigation into the murder. Not yet, anyway. With any luck at all, he wouldn't find out until she had discovered Brian Sutcliffe's killer.

"All right, everyone. Let's get in line. One behind the other, please!"

Grumbling, the ladies obeyed Rita's orders. With much shoving, pushing, and complaining, they finally managed a straggly line in front of the police station where they'd been told to assemble.

"Now," Rita announced, "I'm going to pair you off. Each pair will go in a different direction. You all have your whistles, don't you?"

A few of the women nodded: a couple of them held up the whistles hanging around their necks.

"Just to make sure," Rita insisted, "I want everyone to blow their whistles. Once."

Unfortunately, her last word was drowned out by a chorus of shrill screams from the women's whistles. Jumping up and down,

Rita waved her arms in an attempt to quiet them. No one paid any attention to her. In fact, they seemed determined to outdo each other, blowing until their faces were red.

In the midst of all the horrendous racket, George came running out of the station, with Sid hot on his heels. " 'Ere, 'ere," George yelled, "what's all this then?"

"Crikey!" Sid shouted. "I thought it was the bloomin' invasion."

"Shut up, *shut up!*" Rita screeched, only adding to the noise.

Finally, George went down the line, tugging whistles from the mouths of the grinning women. "It's about time you lot learned to keep order," George grumbled. "This is serious business. One of your members is missing, in the hands of hardened criminals. I should think you'd all be more worried about her than tormenting your leader."

The women sobered at once, exchanging sheepish glances. "Sorry, Rita," Florrie said, always the first to kiss Rita's boots. "We didn't mean no harm."

Red in the face herself, Rita pulled herself up straight as a ramrod. "Now listen to me," she barked. "Nellie's life could depend on how fast we find her. I suggest we get to it and start looking for her." She called off names and gave them the direction in which they had to go.

Marge wasn't too happy to find she was paired with Florrie. She'd have much rather been with her mate, Clara, who wasn't afraid of anything or anyone. Florrie was such a baby, jumping at every little noise and always afraid the Germans were going to come and take her away. Though why on earth the Nazis would want her, Marge couldn't imagine.

She managed to wave to Clara as they set off, happy to notice her friend didn't seem any happier than she was with her partner, Joan Plumstone. Joan was all right, but she hardly ever smiled, and if she ever really laughed she'd crack her face. Clara wouldn't like that. She liked to joke around all the time. Though Marge had to admit, Nellie being missing wasn't much of a joke.

"Come on," she said to Florrie, who looked as if she'd wet her drawers any minute, "we've got a long walk before we get to the woods. We need to hurry."

"I can't hurry too much," Florrie said in her whiney voice. "My feet hurt."

Blimey, they'd barely started and her blinking feet hurt already? Marge heaved a sigh. This was not going to be much fun.

181

Nellie pulled her knees up under her chin and watched the sunlight creeping through the cracks in the barn walls. She'd heard her captors come back hours ago. From what she could hear, their mission, whatever that was, had failed. They would have to try again tonight.

She was hungry and thirsty, and she needed to piddle. The thought of enduring another day and night in this horrible place was enough to drive her barmy. Right now the three of them were sleeping.

When she thought about the lousy night she'd had, trying to sleep on the hard floor, she got really, really mad. Bloody sods. She'd like to ram their teeth down their throat. Her anger goaded her into action. She slid forward until she was close to the edge of the ledge and could look down.

They were right below her, lying on their backs, mouths open, sleeping like babies. Well, she'd settle that. In her temper she kicked a pile of hay over the ledge.

It showered down on the three below. None of them moved. Not even when some of it went in Stan's mouth. He just blew it out with his next breath.

Frustrated and angrier than ever, Nellie eyed the lamp. That would make a nice noise. She picked it up and hurled it to the ground. It landed with an almighty crash and a splintering of glass.

"What the . . . ?" Stan sat up and rubbed his eyes.

Robbie rolled over and stared sleepily at him. "Watcha doing?"

"I didn't do nothing. The lamp fell down." Stan looked up, straight into Nellie's face. "No, it didn't. That bitch threw it down. It could've killed one of us."

"Too bad it didn't," Nellie said nastily.

" 'Ere, watch it. Or I'll come up there and show you what for."

"You and whose bleeding army?"

"Just me, that's who."

"Shut up, Stan. Don't let her lead you on," Jimmy said.

Nellie sat on the edge of the ledge, her legs dangling over their heads. "What makes you think the bobbies are going to mistake you for the musketeers, anyhow? Them blokes are a lot older than you. How old are you anyway? Thirteen?"

Robbie snorted. "We're fifteen, stupid."

"Shut up," Stan warned.

"Fifteen." Nellie shook her head. "Old enough to know better. You're never going to get away with this, you know. The bobbies will know you're not the musketeers. They're a lot more clever than you are. They wouldn't have messed up a mission."

"We didn't mess it up," Robbie muttered. "We couldn't get on the base, that's all."

Both his companions turned on him. "Shut your mouth!" they snarled in unison.

Nellie felt a stab of hope. "Is that your mission? To get on the American base?"

"Never mind what our mission is. Just keep your nose out of it if you don't want it smashed in."

Nellie smiled. "What if I was to tell you I know how to get you on the base?"

All three boys stared up at her. "How'd you know that?" Stan demanded.

Sadie shrugged. "Been on it enough times, haven't I. I know all the tricks. I could get you in and out without anyone knowing you'd been there. That's as long as you didn't mess things up while you was there."

"Why would you want to help us do that?" Stan asked, his voice full of suspicion.

"It's blinking obvious, isn't it. I tell you how to get on the base, and you let me go." She waited, holding her breath, for his answer. If they didn't let her go soon, she didn't know what she was going to do.

Chapter 10

Elizabeth sat at her desk in her office and reached for the telephone. Polly was out collecting the rents, giving her the chance to ring Dr. Sheridan and find out what she could about Brian Sutcliffe's murder. As usual, the doctor was wary about answering her questions.

"All I can tell you," he said, when she'd refused to be deterred from her quest, "is that the knife used to stab the victim had an unusually long blade."

"Yes, the wedding cake knife belonging to Mrs. Crumm," Elizabeth said impatiently. "I already know that. I want to know if there is anything else you can tell me."

"Perhaps you should talk to P.C. Dalrymple."

"I've already talked to George. Now I'm talking to you."

"Well, I suppose it won't hurt anything to tell you that the victim also had a head injury. Though that wasn't what killed him, of course. The knife did that. Went right through the heart." The doctor paused, then added quietly, "I'd say the killer knew exactly the right spot to stab him."

Elizabeth thanked him and hung up the telephone. Now she knew why George suspected Rodney Winterhalter. Surely no one knew how to stab a man through the heart better than a surgeon.

Things looked black for Rodney. He certainly had motive and opportunity. In spite of all that, Elizabeth had a strong feeling that he didn't kill Brian Sutcliffe, and that somewhere in the back of her mind she held the key to the real killer.

She knew from experience that if she left the niggling hunch alone and stopped worrying at it, sooner or later the solution would occur to her. She'd have to trust her instincts and hope that it happened in time to save Rodney from a most unpleasant situation.

Elizabeth was almost at the front door when she heard the telephone ringing again in the kitchen. Her heart jumped, knowing Violet would answer it when she didn't pick up in her office.

Racing across the hallway, she heard the ringing stop and prayed she'd be in time before Violet hung up. "I'm here!" she called out as she ran down the stairs. "Tell whoever it is to hold on!" with her hands raised she pushed the door open and burst into the kitchen.

Violet stood across the room with a smug look on her face, the telephone in her hand. "How'd you know it was him?"

Elizabeth caught her breath. "Who is it?"

"Your major, of course." She held the receiver out to her. "I was just telling him you'd gone out."

Elizabeth made herself walk casually across the kitchen and took the telephone out of Violet's hand. "I thought it might be George again."

Violet grinned. "Yeah, and I thought Father Christmas really flies down the chimney."

Elizabeth made a face at her and spoke into the mouthpiece.

His deep voice chased away all her worries. "I'm fine," he assured her in answer to her anxious question. "Violet said you're having some excitement, though."

She told him about Nellie and the search going on for her.

"I heard the musketeers were on the prowl again," Earl said, when she was finished. "Seems our boys found a Jeep smashed on the beach this morning. Looked like it had been shoved over the cliff."

"Oh, my. Thank heavens it didn't set off a mine. Rita would have had half the village out there defending the beaches against an invasion."

"No kidding. Let's hope the search party finds Nellie today."

"Anyway, I'll be joining the search party later on, but first I want to talk to Dickie Muggins about the murder. It seems he had a violent argument with Brian Sutcliffe the night before the wedding."

"I suppose it's useless to suggest that you let George and Sid conduct that investigation."

"Quite useless."

"That's what I thought. How's it coming along?"

"Well, George seems convinced that Rodney killed Brian, and I have to admit, circumstances do point to him, though there's no proof at all. It's pure conjecture at this point."

"What do *you* think?"

"I don't know." She pondered on that for a moment, then added slowly, "I think I need to ask a few more questions before I make up my mind."

"Well, just be careful, okay?"

"I will if you will."

"I'm always careful."

She smiled. "I wish I could believe that. When will you be coming home, or is that something else you can't tell me?"

There was an odd pause, then he said softly, " 'Home.' That sounds so darn good. Wish I could be there right now."

Aware of Violet bustling around in the background, she said fervently, "Oh, so do I."

"Well, with any luck, it won't be long. One thing I can tell you, I'll be there just as soon as possible."

"I know." She lowered her voice. "I miss you."

"I miss you, too, sweetheart."

She hung up the telephone, her eyes moist. Without looking at Violet she headed for the door. "I'll be back in time for dinner," she said, not trusting her voice to say more.

For once, Violet didn't give her a cheeky reply.

"Come on, Florrie." For the tenth time that morning Marge paused, waiting for Florrie to catch up with her. She was thoroughly fed up. All Florrie had done was whine ever since they started down the trail through the woods. Marge watched her companion trudge slowly toward her, stopping every now and then to wipe her brow.

"I'm thirsty," Florrie complained, "and it's getting hot."

Marge had to agree; it was getting awfully warm and muggy. Unusual for the end of May. Must be a storm coming. "Well, come on, we're almost out of our side of the woods, and Rita said once we get out the other side we should start back to the village."

"It's such a long walk back from here," Florrie moaned. "I'll never get there. Me feet are all blistered."

Marge looked at Florrie's feet. "I'm not surprised. Where on earth did you get those shoes? The rag bag?"

Florrie looked offended. "They're the most comfortable shoes I've got. I've had them for years."

"Bloomin' looks like it, too." Marge started walking again, impatient for the search to be over so she could get back to the tea room and have a currant bun and a nice hot cup of tea. They weren't going to find Nellie in the woods. She was sure of that. It was too easy to get lost in all the trees unless you stuck to the trails, and if she were tied up somewhere, as Rita seemed to think, they'd have surely found her by now.

"Wait for me!" Florrie whined behind her.

Marge stomped on. She wouldn't put it past Nellie to be messing about with them musketeers, having a good time with them, instead of in danger like Rita said. Somehow Nellie being in danger didn't seem real.

War was real. Bombs falling and soldiers fighting and planes going down in the ocean. All that was real. People just didn't go around kidnapping strangers in wartime. There was too much else to worry about. Them musketeers had taken Nellie for a lark, and she was probably back in Bessie's tea room, telling everyone what a good time she had.

Having salved her conscience, Marge was prepared to make straight for the lane that would lead them back to the main road. To heck with plodding through the rest of the woods. Nellie wasn't here, and that was that.

"Come on, Florrie," she called out. "We're going back home." Judging whereabouts the lane would be, she veered off the trail to the right and headed in that direction. It took longer than she thought, and she had to struggle up and down banks, squeeze through shrubbery, and climb over fallen logs before she finally sighted the clearing up ahead.

Lost in her thoughts, she'd forgotten about Florrie, until she turned around and saw no sign of her. "Florrie?" She waited, expecting to hear Florrie's whine, but only the birds twittering in the trees answered her.

"Florrie? *Florrie!*" Cursing under her breath, Marge climbed back up the bank she'd just slid down. Stupid woman. Now she'd have to go back and get her.

It was even harder going back than it had been coming. She had to hunt for the signs of her tracks to make sure she was going in the right direction. All the time she called out Florrie's name, until her voice was hoarse. Squirrels chattered at her, sparrows fluttered out of branches, and crows screeched at her, but no sound of a human voice answered her cries.

It didn't seem possible that the woods were full of people searching for Nellie, and not one of them could hear her. To make matters worse, a faint rumbling of thunder in the distance warned of a storm approaching.

Marge was almost in tears by the time she reached the trail again. Still no sign of Florrie. Stumbling and running, Marge hurried along the trail in the hopes that the silly woman had continued along it. At the pace Florrie was walking, Marge should easily catch up with her. The trail ended, however, without Marge ever seeing another living soul. Thoroughly fed up, she reached the lane and set off for the village.

Either Florrie had gone back the way they'd come, or something bad had happened to her. Now Marge no longer thought Nellie was having a good time with the musketeers. In fact, she was beginning to really worry about her. She was also worried as to how she would explain to Rita that she'd lost Florrie somewhere in the woods.

Elizabeth arrived in North Horsham just before noon. She hadn't rung Dickie Muggins to let him know she was coming. She'd learned that when people are taken by surprise, they reveal much more if they haven't had time to prepare their answers.

To her relief, Dickie was in his studios when she called on him. His assistant, a freckled-faced redheaded woman with the unlikely name of Frenchie, ushered her into a waiting room and handed her a tattered copy of a film magazine.

Elizabeth, preferring live theater to the

cinema, thumbed through it without paying much attention. She was relieved when Dickie came bustling in, wearing a gaudy orange silk shirt with baggy brown trousers. His black scarf floated behind him as he surged forward, his hand extended as if he meant to shake hers.

Holding firmly onto the magazine, Elizabeth rose smoothly to her feet. Now that she knew the truth about the photographer, she found it rather difficult to meet his gaze. "It was kind of you to see me on such short notice, Mr. Muggins," she murmured, as he led her into a tiny office.

The walls were covered with photographs, some in color, most in black-and-white. Weddings, birthday parties, horse races, boating regattas, there seemed no end to the functions this weird little man had attended as official photographer.

"I'm so glad you paid me a visit today," Dickie said, ushering her onto a chair. "I have the proofs of the wedding. I was going to take them into Sitting Marsh, but as long as you're here, would you mind taking them with you? It would save me a trip."

"I'll be happy to take them." Elizabeth waited until he'd handed her the package before saying, "I don't know if you've heard the sad news, but shortly after you left the wedding on Saturday, Brian Sutcliffe was found dead in the cellar of the Sitting Marsh village hall."

Dickie's hand fluttered in front of his face as he uttered a shocked, "Oh, my goodness! Oh, how perfectly dreadful. The poor, poor man. Whatever happened?"

"He was stabbed through the heart," Elizabeth said bluntly.

Dickie staggered, felt for a chair, and sat down on it. "Are you telling me someone *murdered* him? But that's simply ghastly. Oh, dear, oh, dear! Whatever next?"

Elizabeth was far too astute to be swayed by this show of false emotion. "I understand you and Mr. Sutcliffe had a difference of opinion at the Tudor Arms last Friday night."

The photographer's eyes narrowed, and his voice sounded deeper when he answered. "Who told you that, may I ask?"

"It's true, isn't it?"

Dickie made a pretense of brushing something from his sleeve. "We had an altercation, yes. Nothing major. It was all resolved rather quickly."

"I was told you gave Mr. Sutcliffe a warning. I also heard that you were arguing with him in the kitchen shortly before his death."

Dickie's mouth hardened. "If you're suggesting that I killed the man, you couldn't be more wrong. I am well used to intolerant, misinformed people like Brian Sutcliffe. His attacks were nothing new to me. I assure you, if I went around killing everyone who insulted me I'd have an army of deaths on my hands. I am many things, Lady Elizabeth. I'd be the first to tell you that my lifestyle may be controversial, but a murderer? No, indeed not."

"Not even if your lifestyle is threatened?" Elizabeth asked quietly.

Dickie Muggins looked her straight in the eye. "Not even then."

For some reason, she believed him. Picking up her handbag, she said briskly, "Well, I won't take up any more of your time, Mr. Muggins."

She was about to depart when he spoke again. "I'm not the only one who argued with Sutcliffe, you know. If I were you, I'd have a chat with that bridesmaid. The tall one. I had the room next to Sutcliffe, and I heard her cursing him on the landing. Not nice language for a lady to use at all."

Elizabeth paused. "You mean Fiona Farnsworth?"

"I believe that's her name, yes."

"Thank you, Mr. Muggins. I appreciate

your time." She left, frowning. Of course, Fiona had gone to Brian Sutcliffe's room. She had forgotten about that. Goodness, she was letting her worries about Earl and Nellie cloud her brain. It wasn't like her at all to forget something so important during an investigation. Though what Fiona might have to do with Brian Sutcliffe's death was hard to imagine.

"You did *what?*" Rita's yell was even more terrible than Marge had expected. "How could you possibly lose *Florrie?* She's not a *dog,* you know. She didn't just *run off.*"

Marge explained as best she could, while the women who had made it back to the tea shop sat looking at her as if she'd deliberately got Florrie lost. "I went all the way back," she said, looking longingly at the plate of Chelsea buns on Rita's table. "I even went down the trail after her. She just disappeared."

"The musketeers got her," Joan Plumstone muttered.

A chorus of shocked cries turned the heads of nearby customers.

"Shh!" Rita warned. "We don't want to start a panic, for heaven's sake. Florrie just got lost, that's all. Let's wait until the others get back. Maybe she ran into someone out there and is coming back with them. Meanwhile, we have to decide what to do about Nellie if we don't find her today."

"What are the bobbies doing about it?" someone asked.

"God knows." Rita picked up her cup and sipped her tea. "Knowing Sid and George, they're too wrapped up with that murder at the wedding to have time to look for our Nellie."

"What about Lady Elizabeth? Can't she do something about Nellie?"

Rita sniffed. "Apparently her ladyship has better things to do than search for a missing tenant."

"That's not fair," Marge said hotly. "You know she cares about Nellie as much we do. She's most likely trying to find out who killed Brian Sutcliffe. I'd say that's just as important. After all, that poor man is dead."

"How do we know Nellie isn't, too?" Joan said.

Marge felt a stab of fear. "Don't even think that."

"Well," Rita said, "don't worry about Lady Elizabeth. Whatever she can do I can do, and a lot more efficiently at that. If she spent more time worrying about her responsibilities instead of running around after that precious major of hers she'd get a lot more done."

Aware that someone had come up behind Rita, Marge looked at the newcomer. Her eyes widened, and she nudged Rita hard in the shoulder.

Rita shook her off with a testy, "Oh, shut up, Marge. You know I'm right. Her ladyship throws her weight around a lot, but it's yours truly who does all the organizing and getting the job done. We wouldn't have a war effort at all in Sitting Marsh if it weren't for me."

Marge's mouth trembled as she smiled at the woman standing behind Rita's chair. "Good afternoon, your ladyship," she said loudly. "How nice to see you."

As Nellie might have expected, Stan wouldn't let her go, but he had agreed to bring her back food and drink, which was something. She sat waiting impatiently for the three lads to return with the supplies. Stan wouldn't tell her what they planned to do. All she knew was that it had something to do with the American base and that it had to be done at night. She'd refused to give away any of her secrets until she'd had something to eat and drink.

She'd spent the last hour or so working out what she could tell them that would sound like she was helping them but at the same time would get them caught. The thing she was worried about was that they'd get caught and wouldn't tell anyone where she was.

It was obvious from the rusty equipment lying around that the barn wasn't used anymore. So many farm workers had been called up that the farmers were short-handed and had closed off some of their land until the war was over. The Land Army girls did a lot of the work, but there was only so many of them to go around.

Nellie could be dead and gone to heaven by the time someone found her. Maybe if she shouted loud enough, someone working in the fields would hear her.

After several minutes of yelling her head off, her throat was so raw she could hardly swallow. If she didn't get something to drink soon, she was going to die of thirst. Stan had given her a few sips of sour lemonade that hadn't helped her thirst at all.

Somehow she had to find a way to get down and escape from this place. Maybe if she could drop off the ledge and roll on the ground without hurting herself . . .

Nellie was considering the risks when she heard the sound of the Jeep returning. It amazed her that the field workers hadn't noticed the Jeep coming back and forth to the barn. The building itself hid the noisy vehicle from view as it crossed the field, but surely they must have heard the engine. Then again, everyone was used to hearing Jeeps driving around and took no notice of them anymore. Stan was no fool. He'd picked a good spot for his meeting place.

Her need to satisfy her hunger and thirst chased away all thoughts of trying to escape as she waited for the huge barn doors to open. When at last they did, the sunlight almost blinded her.

Blinking, she couldn't see who was in the Jeep at first. The doors grated closed again, and for a moment all she could see were bright spots of light in front of her eyes. Then, gradually, her vision cleared. She heard a whimpering and thought at first the boys had brought back a dog with them. Then she saw the figure being roughly hauled out of the Jeep.

She blinked, and blinked again. "Florrie? Is that you?"

The frightened woman peered up at her, crying, "Nellie! Are you all right? What's going to happen to us?"

201

"Something nasty if you don't shut up wailing," Jimmy said harshly.

Florrie whimpered again.

Jimmy held her hands behind her back, while Robbie dragged the ladder over to the ledge. "Get up there," Jimmy ordered, giving her a shove. "Maybe your mate can keep you quiet."

"I still don't think we should have brought her back here," Robbie said, as Florrie started crawling up the ladder. "Stan ain't going to like it one bit."

"What else was I supposed to do with her?" Jimmy demanded. "Bury her in the woods?"

Florrie squealed and scrambled up the ladder with surprising agility.

Incensed at their treatment of the fragile woman, Nellie glared down at them. "Where is Stan, anyhow? Where is my grub?"

"He's bringing it on his bicycle," Robbie said, as he dragged the ladder away from the ledge again. "He couldn't very well go into the High Street in a Jeep, now, could he."

Nellie was about to answer when one of the doors creaked open a few inches and Stan slipped through the crack. He carried a satchel in his hand, and Nellie prayed he had something to eat and drink in there.

"I thought I told you to wait for me in the woods," he said, scowling at his companions. "I had to bike all the way across that field."

"We couldn't," Jimmy said gruffly. "We ran into a bit of trouble."

Stan swore and dropped the satchel to the ground. "What happened?"

Jimmy jerked a thumb up at the ledge. "That."

Florrie drew back as Stan stared up at them. "Where the hell did she come from?"

"She popped up out of nowhere. We almost ran over her. Then when she saw us she went bananas. Said she knew we'd got Nellie." Jimmy jerked his thumb again. "That's the name of the other one."

Stan lifted both hands and raked them through his hair. "And you brought her back here? Are you bleeding stupid? Now we have to get rid of two of them."

Nellie's stomach turned over. She heard a thump behind her and looked over her shoulder. Florrie was on the floor in a dead faint.

Chapter 11

By the time Elizabeth arrived back in Sitting Marsh it was almost two o'clock. Having missed lunch, which she knew would not sit well with Violet, she decided to stop in Bessie's Tea Shop and enjoy a pot of tea and sandwiches before paying Fiona a visit at Priscilla's flat.

She wasn't too happy to find members of the Housewives League occupying some of the tables when she walked in. Judging from the noise level, something important had happened. Praying that they had found Nellie safe and sound, she resisted the urge to slip out again unnoticed and approached Rita's chair. Just in time to hear the abominable woman make a nasty remark about her relationship with Earl.

She was about to announce her presence, which had already been noticed by Marjorie Gunther, when Rita had the audacity to declare that Elizabeth made no contribution to the war effort.

Ignoring Marge's stuttered greeting, Elizabeth said quietly, "How nice to know the future of our country is in such capable hands. I wonder if Mr. Churchill is aware of Rita Crumm's magnificent contributions to such a worthy cause."

Marge and a few of the others giggled, while Rita had the grace to look embarrassed, though she covered it well. "Lady Elizabeth," she said, rising from her chair. "We were just talking about you."

"So I heard." Elizabeth nodded at the rest of the group. "Please don't get up. I'm only here for a moment. I was wondering if Nellie has been found. I don't see her here."

"Not only has Nellie not turned up, your ladyship," Marge said, earning a scowl from Rita, "but now Florrie's missing, too."

Elizabeth stared at her in alarm. "Great heavens! Are you sure?"

"Quite sure, m'm," Marge assured her. "I was with her when she disappeared."

Elizabeth listened as Marge gave a hurried account of how she'd lost Florrie.

"We're waiting for the rest of them to come back," Rita added when she was finished. "We're hoping she ran into them and is coming back with them."

"Here they come now," Marge said, nodding at the door.

The group of women filing in through

the door looked hot and weary, though they all managed a smile for Elizabeth. Much to her dismay, however, no one had seen any sign of Florrie, and had no idea she was even missing.

"Now what do we do?" Marge demanded, looking hopefully at Elizabeth.

"I'll report Florrie's disappearance to the constables," Elizabeth said, trying to sound calm. Inside she felt anything but calm. Two missing women and a murdered man on her hands. The whole situation was fast reaching disaster proportions. "I'll tell George to let the inspector know what's happening and ask him for help in searching for them. The rest of you start going door to door. Perhaps someone saw or heard something helpful. Report back to me if you hear anything at all. I'll be at Priscilla's flat for a while, or you can ring me up at the manor from the police station."

To Elizabeth's surprise, Rita didn't offer one protest at having matters taken out of her hands. In fact, she seemed almost relieved that she was no longer in charge and responsible for her missing members. She did find the nerve to dismiss her crew with a terse, "All right, you lot. You heard her ladyship. Get going!"

The women scrambled to obey, and as they hurried out the door, Rita added, "I'll ask around the tables here, if you like, Lady Elizabeth."

"That's a good idea, Rita. Thank you." Elizabeth left her to her task, thankful that the dratted woman hadn't made a scene for once.

It took her no more than a minute or two to reach the police station, and she hopped off her motorcycle with less attention than usual to her skirt, which tended to ride up over her knees in a most unbecoming manner when she was in a rush.

Hurrying into the police station, she was rather annoyed to see George lounging back in his chair, one hand holding a sugary Banbury cake, while the other propped up the daily newspaper.

He dropped the cake onto the newspaper when she entered and hastily got to his feet. "Good afternoon, your ladyship. Nice surprise to see you down here. I was just having a spot of afternoon tea."

Sid's voice floated in from the back office. "Caught in the act again, George?"

George scowled. "Shut your mouth, Sid."

Elizabeth let out her breath in exasperation. "I was rather expecting you to be out searching for Nellie Smith," she said, a trifle crossly. "She's been missing for seventeen hours. The Housewives League has been out all morning looking for her."

"I was establishing headquarters here," George said huffily, "to direct operations. If anyone should be out there searching, it should be that lazy bugger in the back room."

"I heard that!" Sid called out. "You told me to stay here and not get in the way."

George cleared his throat. "I take it the young lady has not been found?"

"Not only has Nellie not been found, but Florrie is now missing." Elizabeth looked up at the clock above his head. "I would not like another night to pass before we find them."

George clicked his tongue. "Now how on earth did Florrie go and get lost? Not very considerate of her, when we already have to take care of a murder and one missing person."

"I'm sure she didn't lose herself on purpose, George. I need you to notify the inspector right away and ask for volunteers to help search for the women. Up until now the musketeers have been content with causing damage to property, but things have taken a very nasty turn. We have to assume the worst and act accordingly."

George had been frowning in concentration while she talked, and now he shook his head in confusion. "Act how, your ladyship?"

"Act accordingly!" Sid called out.

Elizabeth laid her hands on the desk and fixed a stern glare on the constable. "Find them, George. As quickly as possible. I don't care how you go about it. Call in the army if you have to, but find them. Now. Today."

"Yes, your ladyship. We'll do our best, I'm sure."

"I'm relying on you, George. You, too, Sid!"

With their chorus of assurances ringing in her ears, Elizabeth rushed out of the station and climbed aboard her motorcycle. One stop to talk to Fiona, then she would head back to the manor and call Earl. He'd know what to do.

To her great relief, Fiona answered her urgent rapping on the door knocker. She was half afraid that Priscilla's friend would be out shopping and she'd have to hunt her down.

Fiona was obviously surprised to see her guest, and somewhat reluctantly invited her in.

Elizabeth could understand why when

she saw the front room. Magazines and books were strewn around; a slipper lay near the door, its partner flung across the room. A half-empty cup of cold tea sat on the table next to the settee, and next to it a plate of broken biscuits nestled among a mound of crumbs.

"Sorry for the mess, your ladyship," Fiona muttered, sweeping a dressing gown and pyjamas up in her arms from the settee. "I wasn't expecting visitors." Priscilla's cat, which had been snuggled up in the clothes, uttered a plaintive meow and leapt to the floor.

Hoping the woman would clean up before the new bride returned home, Elizabeth took the chair she was offered. Declining a cup of tea and a biscuit, she opened the conversation with a safe topic.

"The wedding was quite beautiful," she murmured. "Priscilla looked magnificent."

Fiona sat down nervously on the edge of the settee. "Yes, she did. Pity about the murder, though. Rather spoilt things, didn't it. I'm just glad Prissy got away before it happened."

"Or at least before the body was discovered," Elizabeth amended.

Fiona seemed startled. "You think it happened while she and Wally were still there?"

"Possibly. After all, the knife was missing before the cake was cut."

"Oh, yes, I see what you mean. How dreadful. Thank heavens they didn't know about it then."

"It was fortunate, yes." Elizabeth stared hard at her. "You didn't care for the victim, did you?"

Fiona's fingers clenched and unclenched. "I hardly knew him."

"Oh, really? I was under the impression you knew him rather well." Elizabeth paused, then added deliberately, "You did go to his room at the Tudor Arms with him, didn't you?"

Fiona's face flamed, and she took a moment to answer. "May I ask how you know that?"

"You were seen and heard. The point is, you didn't mention that you knew Brian Sutcliffe when the constable talked to you at the wedding. I can't help wondering why."

Fiona shifted uncomfortably on her seat. "I couldn't say anything in front of Malcolm. He'd have gone berserk. He doesn't often lose his temper, but when he does, he can be quite nasty."

"He didn't know you'd gone to Mr. Sutcliffe's room?"

"No, he didn't. We'd been arguing about getting married that night. He's been bothering me about it a lot lately. I keep telling him I'm not ready to get married again yet, but he won't take no for an answer. He acts as if he owns me and it's my duty to marry him. I had enough of that with my first husband. So that night when Brian started flirting with me, just to show Malcolm I wasn't under his thumb, I flirted back."

"I imagine Malcolm didn't like that at all."

Fiona shrugged. "Malcolm started drinking too much and acting like he didn't care. Then Brian suggested having a drink in his room, so I went with him. Just to teach Malcolm a lesson. That's all."

"I see. Malcolm didn't see you leave?"

"No, he didn't. Which made me mad. It was all for nothing."

"How do you know he didn't see you leave with Mr. Sutcliffe?"

"Because the next morning at the church he asked me where I went. The last thing he remembered was looking around for me and I wasn't there. I told him I got disgusted with him and came back here. I didn't want him making a scene at the wedding."

Elizabeth nodded. "I can understand that. So you went up to Mr. Sutcliffe's room."

Fiona paused, looking down at her hands. "Yes. I regretted it the minute he closed the door behind us. In spite of how Malcolm is, I really love him, and I knew I'd made a big mistake. I told Brian that, and tried to leave, but he got nasty and told me it was too late to change my mind. He grabbed hold of me but I managed to get away and got out the door. He followed me but I told him if he didn't leave me alone Malcolm would —" She broke off and stared at Elizabeth. "Malcolm never knew about Brian," she added finally. "I never told him. When I found out Brian was dead, there was no need to tell him."

"Did you speak to Mr. Sutcliffe at the wedding?"

Fiona shuddered. "No, I didn't. I stayed as far away from him as I could get."

"And Malcolm didn't speak to him?"

"I don't think Malcolm knew who he was. At least, he didn't seem to recognize him at the wedding." Fiona met Elizabeth's gaze. "If you're thinking that Malcolm might have had something to do with Brian's murder, then you're looking at the wrong person. Malcolm's not a killer. I'd stake my life on it."

Elizabeth rose to her feet. "I certainly hope you're right." She thanked the woman and left, still not wholly convinced by what she had heard. She couldn't help thinking there was something she was missing, but she still couldn't put her finger on it. It annoyed her greatly when that happened.

To her dismay, when she started back to the manor, large drops of rain splattered on her hat. Huge flashes of lightning lit up the sky over the ocean, and the ominous roll of thunder promised a nasty storm on the way.

Elizabeth zoomed up the hill, anxious now to speak with Earl again. Since the musketeers had apparently stolen two Jeeps, perhaps he could spare some men to help search for the culprits and hopefully find the missing women.

Polly was in the office when she went in and looked up with an expression of relief. "We was getting worried about you, m'm. Violet was really put out when you didn't turn up for lunch."

Elizabeth smiled. "Don't worry about Violet, Polly. I've had a word with her and she's forgiven me. Especially when she heard the news about the kidnapping."

Polly frowned. "You mean about Nellie? But I thought she already knew about that."

"I'm talking about Florrie Evans." Elizabeth sat down at her desk and started sorting through the post that Polly had left for her. "She was helping in the search this morning and now she's missing as well."

Polly let out a shocked cry. "What's happening to everyone? Is it the musketeers?"

"We're not really certain about that." Elizabeth did her best to reassure the frightened girl. "I'm going to call the American base and ask for help in searching for them. I'm quite sure they'll be found safe and sound before too long."

Polly's eyes were wide and scared. "What if them blokes killed them and buried them somewhere? We might never find them. What if the musketeers are going around killing all the women? None of us will be safe!"

"That's nonsense," Elizabeth said firmly. "I'm sure there is a simple explanation for Florrie's disappearance."

"But they did take Nellie," Polly insisted. "Sadie said the Housewives League saw them."

"Well, yes, but I'm sure they meant no

real harm. They've never hurt anyone before."

"There's always a first time." Polly sat
hugging herself as if she were cold. "I'm
scared, m'm. I'm really scared."

Elizabeth abandoned the bills for the
moment. "Polly, why don't you just go
home and be with your mother. It's almost
time to leave anyway, and there's a bad
storm on the way. You'll feel safer once
you are home. I'm sure by the morning
we'll have some news and all this will be
over." She was sure of no such thing, but it
felt good to say the words.

Polly looked somewhat relieved. "Oh,
can I? I would feel better, I know."

"Of course. Just leave what you're doing.
It can wait until tomorrow."

She waited for Polly to leave the room,
then reached for the telephone. She badly
needed to talk to Earl. Not only to ask for
his help, but just to hear his voice. His
quiet strength always seemed to steady her
in times of turbulence, and she needed him
now as she never had before.

She had to wait for some time before the
ringing was answered at the base. The
stern voice that spoke to her informed her
that Major Monroe was unavailable. With
a deepening feeling of dread, she replaced

the receiver. How she hated those words and what they conveyed. Now she had to suffer another night of torment before she knew he was safe again. What's more, at least another night would pass before she could ask for his help in finding Florrie and Nellie. She could only hope it wouldn't be too late.

Polly ran down the steps and hurried around the corner to the stables where she had left her bicycle. She wasn't going to feel safe until she was in her own bedroom, surrounded by all her pictures of her favorite film stars on the walls. How she wished Marlene would come home. She missed her sister more than she ever thought she would.

A voice called out behind her, making her jump. "Where are you going in such a blinking hurry?"

"Sadie!" She swung around, trying hard not to burst into tears. "Have you heard the news? Florrie Evans has disappeared."

"Blimey." Sadie shifted the bulging shopping bag she carried to the other hand. "Who's going to be next?"

"That's what I'd like to know." Polly wheeled her bicycle out under the black sky. The rain was pattering down steadily now. She was going to be soaked by the time she got home.

Sadie frowned at her. "Is anyone looking for her? They never found Nellie, did they?"

"No, they didn't. I don't think they're going to find Florrie, neither. Lady Elizabeth said she was going to ask the base if they could send some of their boys to look for them both."

Sadie frowned. "I'm going to help look for them, too. The more people looking for them, the more likely we'll find them."

Polly swallowed. Sadie was awfully brave. She wished she were as brave as that. "Where will you look?"

Sadie put the shopping bag on the ground and rubbed her arms. "Well, I'd start with the old windmill. That'd be a good place to hide someone."

"But you saw the Jeep go into the woods. That's miles from the old windmill."

"A Jeep can go miles, silly, can't it?"

Polly's stomach quivered. "What if you did find them there? They'd get you, too."

"Not if they didn't see me. Once I knew they were there I'd go back and get the bobbies, wouldn't I. I'm not daft."

"You're not going alone, are you?"

Sadie smiled. "Think about it. All those

women tramping about in groups, talking and carrying on? That lot never did know how to keep quiet. Of course they didn't find no one. They heard them coming, didn't they. Now if there's only one person out there . . ." She looked hopefully at Polly. "Or maybe two."

Polly's stomach took a nosedive. "If you think I'm going with you out there you can blinking think again. I hate going out in a thunderstorm."

"It'll be over in a little while. We can go when it moves off."

"It's dangerous out there with them musketeers running around kidnapping everyone. I'm going home. Where it's safe." She pushed her bicycle past Sadie and swung her leg across the saddle.

"Nellie would be out looking for you if you was missing," Sadie called out after her.

No she wouldn't, Polly thought fiercely. Nellie was only interested in meeting GIs. She pedaled furiously down the drive in the rain, more angry at herself than at anyone else. The truth was, she felt ashamed of being such a sissy. Sadie was going to be out there all by herself. What if something happened to her? Polly caught her bottom lip between her teeth. It would be all her fault. She'd never forgive herself.

Polly let the bicycle freewheel while she fought her conscience. It was no good. She couldn't let Sadie go out there on her own. She'd worry herself sick about her. Although the fluttering in her stomach got worse at the thought of what she was about to do, she deliberately swung the front wheel of her bicycle around and pedaled slowly back to the manor.

Chapter 12

Nellie broke off a piece of the pork pie she was holding and held it out to Florrie. "Here, eat this. You'll feel better."

Florrie shook her head, her arms hugging her stomach. "I couldn't eat a thing. If I do I'll bring my breakfast up. I don't know how you can eat anything with death staring us in the face." Her lips trembled and silent tears rolled down her ashen face.

Nellie shoved the piece of pork pie in her mouth and chewed with relish. "If you were as hungry as I am you'd eat it," she said when she'd swallowed it down. "I haven't eaten anything since supper last night. And I ate that early because of Rita's stupid invasion watch. If it hadn't been for her and her bloody Germans we wouldn't be here now."

Florrie moaned. "She'll be so devastated to have our deaths on her conscience."

Nellie opened a bottle of lemonade and offered it to Florrie, who shook her head with a shudder. "We're not going to die, silly. They're just a bunch of soppy school-kids. They're not going to kill us."

221

Florrie stared at her. "I thought they was the musketeers."

Nellie laughed. "Don't let the musketeers hear you say that. They'd be really insulted."

"But they kidnapped us."

"Yeah, 'cos they didn't know what else to do. They got in a panic, that's all."

"They're not going to just let us go."

"I think they will once they do what they came to do."

Florrie looked really scared. "And what's that?"

"I don't know. All I know is they want to get on the base. I said I'd help them if they brought me something to eat and drink."

"You're not going to help them, are you!?"

Nellie almost laughed at Florrie's shocked expression. "Nah, silly. I'm just going to pretend to help them. I'll tell them how to get onto the base without being seen, but I'll really be sending them right into the arms of the MPs."

"How're you going to do that?"

Nellie swallowed more pork pie. "I haven't exactly worked that out yet."

Florrie looked fearfully over the ledge. "Where do you think they've gone?"

Nellie shrugged. "Don't know. I just

hope they stay away until I've come up with a good plan. They're really stupid. It shouldn't be hard to get them caught."

"They were clever enough to steal two Jeeps from under the noses of the Americans," Florrie reminded her.

"Yeah, I don't know how they did that. Someone must have left them outside the base." Nellie tipped the lemonade bottle to her lips and took several gulps. "They were stupid enough to go off and leave us alone up here, though, weren't they."

"They know we can't jump down there." Florrie pointed to the ground below. "We'd break our necks."

"Per'aps." Nellie finished the pork pie, then brushed the crumbs from her fingers. She got to her feet, wincing as her muscles reminded her of the hours she'd spent lying on the hard floor.

She studied the drop below. It had to be at least twenty feet. Maybe she could lower Florrie closer to the ground. Nah. Even if she hung by her feet, which would be quite a trick, and held Florrie's hands, there'd still be too much of a drop.

There wasn't even a rope or anything to use to climb down. She'd searched every inch of the loft. No, the boys knew what they were doing when they'd made them climb up there. She'd just have to find another way to outwit them.

"I wonder if they're still looking for you," Florrie said. "I bet they don't even know I'm missing."

"They must know by now." Nellie could tell by the way the sunlight crept down the cracks in the walls that it was late afternoon. "I wish I had a watch. I hate not knowing what time it is."

"Well, it's not going to make any difference to us soon, is it."

Nellie's patience finally gave out. "Shut up whining, Florrie! They're not going to kill us, so there. The worst they'll do is leave us here to rot after they've done what they came to do on the base."

Just as she said it a crackle of thunder made them both jump.

Florrie uttered a little shriek. "Oh, my, oh, my!"

"Don't worry. I'm not going to let that happen," Nellie said firmly. "I'll find a way to get us out of here. Just let me think about it for a while." She sat down, trying not to let on how scared she felt inside. Right then she couldn't see any way to escape. Even if she could come up with a plan to get the boys caught, there was no guarantee it would work. Or even if it did, there was no way of knowing if the boys would let on about where she and Florrie were. Things weren't looking too bright at all.

It wasn't until late that evening that Elizabeth remembered the proofs still tucked into her handbag. She'd meant to leave them at Priscilla's flat with Fiona, but the news of Florrie's disappearance had thrust it from her mind.

Annoyed with herself for her befuddled state of late, she took out the photographs and eagerly looked through them. She found what she was looking for almost at once. A shot of her and Earl, standing side by side, toasting each other with glasses of champagne in their hands.

They were smiling at each other, a private moment that had been caught by Dickie Muggins's shrewd eyes and recorded for posterity. Feeling more than a little guilty, Elizabeth slipped the proof into her desk drawer. Priscilla would not miss that one, she reassured herself. Neither she nor Wally were in the picture.

Quickly she thumbed through the rest of them. Both she and Earl were in several of the candid shots of the guests, but at a distance, and not noticeable at all. Perhaps later on she would ask Dickie to print an enlargement from the proof she'd kept, and she would have it framed as a gift for Earl.

She studied a picture of guests, helping themselves to food from the long table with the wedding cake in the background. There was Malcolm and Fiona, laughing together, and on the other side of the table was Rodney saying something in his wife's ear. Daphne didn't appear too happy with what he had to say. A fierce frown marred her face, and her hunched shoulders suggested she was agitated about something. Remembering Rodney's mention of Daphne's headache that evening, she wondered again if they'd been arguing.

The finished photographs would look so much better than the proofs. The dull finish would be brighter, and the faces so much more distinct. Absently she brushed at the picture with her thumb. The white specks she'd noticed on Rodney's shoulder didn't budge. Apparently they were embedded in the print.

She thought again about the conversation she'd had with the Winterhalters later that evening. Remembering something else that had been said, she studied Daphne's face more closely. The woman did look rather agitated. Of course. Now she knew what it was that had been bothering her all along.

She glanced up at the clock. Violet had told her the Winterhalters were in the library playing cards. She got up and hurried out to the landing. The door of the Winterhalters' room was a little way down on the left. Reaching it, she tapped lightly on the door.

After waiting a moment or two, she tapped again, louder this time, just in case Daphne was taking a nap. When still no one answered her, Elizabeth carefully opened the door and peeked inside. To her relief the room was empty.

It took her only a moment to reach the wardrobe and open it. The suit that Rodney had worn to the wedding hung next to his wife's bridesmaid gown. Quickly Elizabeth examined the suit. The shoulders were clean.

Frowning, she examined the floor of the wardrobe. Not even a speck of dust. Sadie did her job well. She must remember to praise the girl. Disappointed, she rose to her feet. She was about to close the wardrobe door when an idea occurred to her.

She bent her knees once more and reached for a leg of Rodney's trousers.

Folding back the turnup, she found what she was looking for — tiny specks of colored confetti. The confetti that supposedly had been missing until *after* the Winterhalters had left the village hall. The same confetti that had been sprinkled all over Brian Sutcliffe's body.

"Why are we going out so late?" Polly asked nervously. "It's going to be dark soon."

Pedaling alongside her on the coast road, Sadie took a hand off a handlebar to push her hair out of her eyes. "You wanted to make sure the storm was over, didn't you? Besides, we're going to need the dark to sneak in and rescue the girls."

"That's if we find them." Polly chewed her bottom lip. The closer they got to the windmill, the less she wanted to be there. She hoped Sadie knew what she was doing. "What if the bobbies have already searched the windmill and found no one there?"

"Then we look somewhere else. It's just a first place to start looking."

"But if it's dark, how are we going to see them without lights?"

"I brought a torch with me, didn't I."

"But —"

Sadie twisted her head to look at her.

"Polly, if you're having second thoughts about this then you'd better go home. I don't need to be worried about you as well as the musketeers."

Polly swallowed hard. "I'm not having second thoughts. I just want to know what to expect, that's all."

"If I knew that we'd have nothing to worry about," Sadie said grimly. "Just be prepared for anything."

That did nothing to calm Polly's fears. Her stomach was churning like a keg of butter by the time they reached the turn. The sun had just about disappeared behind the trees, but she could see the top of the windmill sticking up on the hill. "What if they see us coming?"

"They won't know we're looking for them, will they." Sadie swung into the lane. "Besides, if they do, they'll come to us and we won't have to go looking for them."

Polly uttered a squeak of fright. "Then they'll capture us, too!"

"Not if I attack them with this." Sadie pointed to the heavy torch in the basket hooked on the front of her bicycle. "I'll bash them on the head with it."

Polly stopped pedaling. "What am I supposed to do, then?"

"Kick 'em where it hurts." Sadie drew

away from her, pedaling even faster. "Hit 'em with a stick. Between us we should be able to beat them off."

Polly gulped. Now she was really scared. She wished she hadn't eaten bangers and mash for supper. They weren't sitting well in her stomach.

"Come on!" Sadie waved at her and drew even farther away.

Sending up a silent prayer, Polly pedaled furiously to catch up. It was hard to do while they were going uphill, and Sadie reached the clearing to the windmill a while before Polly came to a halt.

"I'm going over there," Sadie said quietly, as Polly leaned her bicycle against a tree. "I can't see any movement, but they could be lying low. You stay here and wait for my signal. Find a big stick, and if you hear a rumpus you come running, all right?"

"No, I'm not all right," Polly said, and crossed her knees. "I've got to piddle."

"Well, go behind a tree. There's no one to see you, is there."

"All right," Polly muttered, still feeling anything but. She watched her friend creep around the edge of the clearing. When Sadie was at the back of the windmill she gave Polly a final wave then crept forward until she disappeared from view.

Polly searched around for a big stick, wondering how on earth she'd ended up in this dangerous situation. They should have asked George if he'd looked in the windmill. She'd told Sadie that, but Sadie had insisted they do it themselves. George would only muck it up, she'd said. Right then, Polly wasn't sure she and Sadie would do any better.

She picked up a likely looking stick and tested it against the palm of her hand. It snapped with a loud crack and she jumped a foot in the air. If anyone was going to muck things up, she thought mournfully, it was going to be her and Sadie. She should never have agreed to come with her. She should have gone and told Lady Elizabeth what Sadie was going to do. She would have known how to stop her.

She discarded the broken stick and looked for another one. After a while she found a short, thick branch that had broken off of a beech tree. This one seemed more sturdy. Grasping it in her hand, she crept back to her lookout spot.

Her stomach flipped over when she saw Sadie in the entrance to the windmill, staring in her direction and jumping up and down waving her arms. Without stopping to think, Polly charged forward, brandishing the branch above her head and yelling, "Let go of her, you rotten buggers!"

She was almost up to her friend when it occurred to her that Sadie was alone and not struggling with the musketeers as she'd imagined. Feeling really stupid, she lowered her arm and slowed her pace.

"What'd you do that for?" Polly demanded, as she came up to the door.

"For God's sake shut up!" Sadie shoved her finger on Polly's lips. "They'll hear you a mile away! I'm going up top to have a look around. You wait here. If you hear me yell, come running."

Polly nodded, shivering with fright. The rickety steps up to the top of the windmill were broken and even missing in places. The thought of rushing up there scared her to death. She'd rather face ten musketeers than go up those steps.

She watched Sadie climb up slowly, testing each step before she trod on it. Polly held her breath and wondered how on earth she would catch Sadie if she fell. The buxom housemaid was twice her weight.

The steps creaked and cracked like gunshots going off, and Polly jumped with each one. Sadie, however, showed no fear and climbed purposefully on until she was out of sight. Polly hung grimly onto the stick and prayed she wouldn't have to use it.

All the excitement had brought back the urge to piddle. She should have gone behind the tree when she had the chance, like Sadie said. She'd forgotten about it while she was searching for the stick, but now she really needed to go.

She hopped around from one foot to the other, willing Sadie to come down before she wet her drawers. She thought about calling up to her friend, but if the musketeers were lurking around somewhere they might hear her and come running. They could overpower her long before Sadie got down from the steps.

Finally she could hold it no longer. She looked around, but the thought of what her mother would say if she knew she'd piddled on the windmill floor drove her outside. She had to sprint right across the clearing to reach the trees. Even then, she couldn't find one big enough to hide her if someone was in the windmill looking out at her.

Stumbling along at a crossed-legged run, she plunged deeper into the woods, where the tree trunks were wider and thick tangled blackberry bushes grew underneath them. At last she spotted the perfect place and squatted down between a withered old oak tree and a bunch of flowery ferns.

The relief of finally letting go made her forget everything else for the moment. It was so peaceful there in the woods. The blackbirds were singing their evening song, and the wind in the branches above her head sounded like the sea. Right in front of her, blue and yellow wildflowers grew in dense clumps. She should take some home to Ma, she thought. Her mother loved flowers.

Polly was about to gather some when she caught sight of the stick she'd dropped in her haste to get behind the bushes. Sadie. Crikey. What if she was calling for help?

With a surge of guilt, she snatched up the stick and galloped back through the trees to the clearing. Caution made her pause at the edge of the woods, and she stared hard at the tall wooden structure of the windmill.

There was no movement, no sound. She might as well be all alone out there. It was getting dark. She could barely make out the doorway now. The fear rushed back, and she raced for the windmill and tumbled inside.

It was even darker in there, and it took her a moment to adjust her eyes. There was no sign of Sadie. Polly tilted her head to listen. She couldn't hear a bloomin' thing. No creaks to tell her Sadie was coming back down the steps. What the flipping heck was taking her so long?

She waited a few more minutes, her concern growing into full-fledged panic. Something was wrong. Sadie should have been back down ages ago. There was nothing for it; she'd have to go up there and look for her.

Gripping her stick, Polly advanced to the steps. The first one made a snapping noise when she trod on it and she whimpered. She couldn't do it. She couldn't climb all the way up there in the dark.

In a wavering voice she called out, "Sadie? Are you all right? Come down! It's dark down here!"

No answer floated down to her and she raised her voice, louder with each call. "Sadie? *Sadie?* Sa-*day!*"

Something scuttled away in the dark and Polly screamed. The shrill sound echoed around the lofty walls and up the stairs. It was the final straw. Polly bolted out of there, across the clearing, grabbed her bicycle, and pedaled like mad back to the road. She was never going back to that horrible place. Someone else would have to rescue Sadie.

Elizabeth found both Rodney and Daphne in the library. Rodney sat playing Patience with the cards, while Daphne seemed engrossed in a book. She soon put it down, however, when Elizabeth entered the quiet room.

"Have you heard from the inspector?" she asked, as Rodney rose to his feet.

Elizabeth settled on a Queen Anne chair and shook her head. "Not yet, I'm afraid."

Rodney sat down again with a thump. "I don't suppose you've found out who killed Sutcliffe," he said, a resigned tone.

"I'm getting closer." Elizabeth hesitated, then asked quietly, "Rodney, when did you learn that Brian Sutcliffe had taken another woman to his room at the Tudor Arms?"

Rodney raised his eyebrows. "When Tess told the constable that night. We were all there. We all heard her tell him about it."

Daphne shot a frightened glance at her husband. "Yes, that's right. That's when we found out."

"But you knew before that, didn't you?" Elizabeth looked hard at Rodney. "I believe you referred to him as a two-timing fortune hunter. You were referring to the incident that upset Tess so much, were you not?"

Daphne's gaze flicked back and forth between her husband and Elizabeth, while Rodney began blustering.

"Not at all. The man was only interested in our daughter because of her financial status. I spoke the truth. That doesn't mean —"

"Then perhaps you can explain the presence of confetti in the turnups of your trousers? All the confetti had been locked up in the basement until some time after you left the village hall."

Rodney's gaze turned frosty. "I think the more relevant question is, your ladyship, how you happen to know there is confetti in my trousers."

Elizabeth straightened her back. "You asked me to investigate the murder. That's exactly what I was doing. I must confess, I'm beginning to wonder if you asked me to do so in the hopes that I would muddle things up and confuse the police to cover up the fact that both you and your wife know more about the death of Brian Sutcliffe than you're willing to admit."

The silence stretched several seconds

while Elizabeth waited for his answer. She hated to think the Winterhalters were involved. It would be a terrible homecoming for Priscilla to discover that her sister and brother-in-law were responsible for a man's death. Yet right now she could see no other explanation for what she had discovered, and, judging from Rodney's silence, it seemed she was right.

Chapter 13

"All right," Rodney said, breaking the silence at last. "You're right, Lady Elizabeth. I saw Tess rush into the kitchen and she was obviously upset. I followed her in and heard her yelling at Sutcliffe. She was accusing him of cheating on her with another woman."

"Rodney —" Daphne began, but he held up his hand.

"No, let me finish. I hid behind the door because I didn't want to embarrass my daughter. I heard her slam the cellar door shut and run out. Sutcliffe was banging on the door so I guessed she'd locked him in. I was furious with him and wanted to give him a piece of my mind. I unlocked the door and saw he had a knife in his hand. I reacted without thinking. I punched him in the jaw and knocked him down the stairs. He was holding a box of confetti in the other hand. Some of it must have sprayed over me."

Daphne moaned. "He must have stabbed himself when he fell."

"He couldn't have," Rodney said shortly.

"The knife fell out of his hand at the top of the stairs. I saw it lying there when I left."

"Locking the door behind you," Elizabeth said quietly.

Rodney looked startled. "No, I don't think I even stopped to close the door. I was so enraged and worried about my daughter. All I could think about was finding her to see if she was all right. The knife had unnerved me. I didn't know she'd threatened him with it."

"Then if you didn't lock the door again, I wonder who did."

"I locked the door," Daphne said, her voice quivering.

Rodney uttered an exclamation and stared at his wife.

"Of course. You knew about the other woman, too," Elizabeth said. "Which is why you called him a cheat and a liar the other night."

"Yes." Daphne looked down at her hands twisting in her lap. "I saw Rodney go into the kitchen, and a moment or two later Tess came out looking upset. I thought she'd been arguing with her father, so I went to the kitchen to find out what had happened. I was just in time to see Rodney punch Brian in the face. I left before he saw me. I didn't want him to know I'd seen what he'd done. But then, later on, I began to worry about Brian. So I went back to the kitchen to see if he was all right."

Rodney muttered something under his breath.

"I'm sorry, darling," Daphne said quickly, "but if the man was hurt I didn't want you to get into trouble for it. I couldn't see anything from the top of the stairs, so I went down there."

She shuddered, and tears started rolling down her face. "I could see he was dead," she said, her voice hushed. "The knife was sticking out of his chest and there was blood everywhere. I thought he'd fallen on the knife when he tumbled down the steps. I knew Rodney would get the blame for his death. Everyone would think he did it on purpose."

She paused while she hunted for a handkerchief in her sleeve, dabbed at her eyes, and blew her nose. "I locked the door and tried to put the key on the shelf to hide it," she continued, while Rodney seemed transfixed, his gaze pinned to his wife's face. "I thought if the body wasn't found until after we'd gone, no one would suspect Rodney. I couldn't quite reach the shelf and the key fell into the milk. I went out and found Rodney and told him I had a headache. By then the speeches were nearly over, so we left."

"Why didn't you tell me?" Rodney almost shouted. "Did you really think I'd stoop to murder? Sutcliffe wasn't worth that."

"I thought it was an accident." Daphne began to sob in earnest. "But his death would have been your fault."

"Oh, good Lord." Rodney buried his head in his hands.

Elizabeth stared thoughtfully at him. "You are absolutely certain the knife was at the top of the stairs when Brian Sutcliffe fell."

"Absolutely." Rodney groaned and raised his head. "Why do you think I've been so worried about my daughter? I can't help wondering if she went back and finished the job after I left."

"It's a possibility," Elizabeth said slowly. "There's one person I haven't spoken to about all this. And it's just occurred to me that I should." She got to her feet. "Try not to worry too much. I think we should be able to clear this up fairly soon, if I'm right."

Rodney rose, too, his eyes full of hope. "Right about what?"

"I'd rather not say at this point." Elizabeth touched Daphne briefly on the shoulder. "I promise to tell you just as soon as I have it sorted out."

Daphne nodded and blew her nose again.

"I appreciate your efforts, Lady Elizabeth," Rodney said, as he walked with her to the door. "If there's anything I can do, please let me know. I'm anxious to see a solution to this, for many reasons."

"I'm sure you are." Elizabeth paused in the doorway. "I'll do my best to get this settled just as soon as possible." She left, hoping she could keep her word. The Winterhalters deserved some peace after all they'd gone through.

She was crossing the hall when the bell at the front door started chiming. Martin was probably already in bed, and Violet was in the kitchen. Since she was right on top of the door, she reasoned, she might as well open it.

Surprised to see Polly there, she opened the door wider, her smile fading when the girl almost fell into the hallway, gasping something she couldn't understand.

"Calm down, Polly," she said as she closed the door again. "Tell me what's happened."

"They've got her," Polly said, fighting for breath. "I . . . couldn't find . . . her."

"Couldn't find who, dear?"

"Sadie!" Polly waved a hand in front of her face and took a huge gulp of air. "She disappeared. Just like the others."

Frowning, Elizabeth shook her head. "But she's here, isn't she? She usually lets us know if she's going out."

"No, m'm. We went to the windmill to look for Nellie and Florrie and Sadie climbed all the way to the top and I had to piddle and when I came back Sadie was gone and —"

"For heaven's sake, child, take another breath." Elizabeth fought to calm her own sense of panic. "Did you talk to George yet?"

"No, m'm. I came straight here. I didn't even tell me mum yet."

"All right, you get on home and let your mother know you're all right, and I'll go down to George's house and alert him."

"I can't go home till I know what happened to Sadie, m'm," Polly wailed. "I want to come with you. It's all my fault. I left her alone up there."

"I'm quite sure Sadie is all right," Elizabeth said, not at all sure about anything. "She might have missed you in the dark and got worried about you, too."

"Oh, I hope so," Polly moaned. "I'll

never forgive meself if something happens to her. That's why I went with her in the first place."

"Well, you were very silly, both of you." Elizabeth headed out the door with Polly hot on her heels. "You shouldn't have gone out alone knowing those hoodlums are on the prowl out there. Especially since we don't know what happened to Nellie and Florrie."

Polly began to sniffle, and Elizabeth mentally chastised herself for being so insensitive. The truth was, she was greatly concerned about Sadie's disappearance. If there was one person she thought she could count on to take care of herself, it was the tough East Londoner. The Cockneys had a reputation for being fearless and indestructible. If Sadie had fallen into the clutches of those criminals, what chance did the rest of the females in the village have to defend themselves?

"You'd better ride in the sidecar," Elizabeth said, as she wheeled her motorcycle out of the stables. "You can tell me if I'm straying off the road. This dratted blackout makes it impossible to get around after dark."

Still sniffing, Polly scrambled into the cramped sidecar and clung to the sides.

245

She looked scared, but determined, which Elizabeth rather admired. The girl had some pluck, she'd give her that.

She drove far more carefully than usual down the hill to George's cottage. Even so, the ride was far from comfortable. There was no moon to light the way, and more than once Polly called out a warning that they were too close to the ditch.

At last they reached the lane that led to George's cottage, and rather than risk taking the motorcycle down there in the dark, Elizabeth left it parked at the end of the lane. Polly kept close to her side and they walked briskly to the path that led up to George's front door.

At one time there had been a wrought-iron gate across the front of the garden, but the War Office had taken all the wrought iron in the village away to use in the airplane factories. Elizabeth sorely lamented their disappearance.

George's wife, Millie, opened the door in answer to Elizabeth's knock. She seemed startled to see her guests and immediately called out to her husband. "George? Her ladyship's here to see you!"

George appeared a minute later, looking somewhat disheveled. He wasn't in uniform and had obviously pulled on a suit coat rather hastily, since the collar was tucked inside and his tie was askew.

"Sadie's gone," Elizabeth said, before he could speak. "That's three women, George. Now, what are you going to do about it?"

George fumbled with his tie. "I'll get me bicycle and be right with you, your ladyship."

"No time for that. I have my motorcycle at the end of the lane. You can ride in the sidecar, Polly can sit behind me, and we'll go back to the place where Sadie was last seen."

Polly looked even more scared, while George exchanged glances with his wife. "If it's all right by you, your ladyship," he said, "I'd rather go on me bicycle."

"No, it's not all right with me. I need you to come with me right now."

"You'd better go, dear," Millie said, giving her reluctant husband a little push.

"If I don't come back," George told her grimly, "you know where the wills are kept."

Polly uttered a faint squeal, while Elizabeth swung around and hurried back down the path. "Come on, both of you. We're wasting time!"

It took several moments to get George squished into the sidecar. Elizabeth then climbed aboard and beckoned to Polly to hop up behind her on the saddle. She could feel the child's body shivering as she wrapped both arms around Elizabeth's waist.

"Where are we going?" George shouted rather belatedly as the motorcycle's engine shattered the peace of the quiet countryside.

"To the windmill!" Elizabeth shouted back.

George yelled something back she couldn't hear, but he didn't sound too pleased. That was possibly due to the problem she was having keeping the motorcycle moving in a straight line. George's weight in the sidecar, added to Polly's reluctance to lean with the motorcycle, made the machine a trifle unwieldy.

"Ditch!" Polly yelled in her ear.

Elizabeth twisted the handlebars, sending the motorcycle across to the other side of the road. "Sorry!" she called out, once she had control of the vehicle again. "It's a little tricky riding this thing without lights."

George yelled again, but she still couldn't hear him. She leaned toward him as far as she dared. "What?"

The dratted machine swerved again and

Polly yelped. Elizabeth fought to right it, letting out a sigh of relief when they were going straight once more.

"I can't hear you, George," she shouted. "You'll have to speak up!"

"He said to turn on the lights!" Polly screeched in her ear.

"But what about the blackout? It's against the law to run with lights!"

George yelled again.

"What did he say?" Elizabeth called out to Polly.

Polly yelled back. "He said to hell with the bloody law!"

"Well, really!" Elizabeth sent George a scandalized glance.

George answered with yet another bellow.

"He says it's an emergency," Polly shouted. "He says we'll be killed if you don't use the lights. I left out the swear words, m'm."

"Thank you, Polly. I heard him this time." Elizabeth found the switch and turned on the headlight. A beam of white light swept up the road ahead of her, nearly blinding her with the contrast.

"Blimey!" Polly yelled. "I'd forgotten how bright that is. Hope there's no Germans flying overhead!"

"If there are," Elizabeth called back,

"we'll have George to thank for our demise." Concentrating now on getting to the windmill as fast as she could without spilling them all onto the road, she opened up the throttle and swept up the coast road. Her turn into the lane caused a moment of panic when the sidecar brushed against the hedge and bounced along the grass verge before she found the pavement again.

George yelled something and Elizabeth called out to Polly.

"What did he say?"

"You don't want to know, m'm," Polly called back.

Elizabeth allowed herself a faint smile. There was no doubt George was having a rough ride, but if it meant finding Sadie and the other two women before harm came to them, she was quite sure he would forgive her.

Her smile faded. That was *if* they found them. The more time that went by, the harder it would be. Something told her it had to be tonight, or they might not see Sadie, Nellie, or Florrie again.

"I spy with my little eye something beginning with *F*."

Nellie stretched her legs out in front of

250

her and groaned. "I'm getting tired of this silly game. I'm hungry, too. I've had nothing but a pork pie since last night."

"P'raps they'll bring some food back with them when they come back," Florrie said hopefully.

"Don't bet on it." Nellie started drumming her heels on the wooden floorboards to get the circulation back in her legs. "Now they got what they wanted from me, I wouldn't be surprised if they don't come back."

"They've got to come back." Florrie pointed to the ground below. "They left their bicycles here. I don't think they're going to drive a Jeep all the way back to North Horsham."

Nellie stared at her. "How'd you know they come from North Horsham?"

Florrie looked smug. "I heard the ginger-haired one say they'd need the bicycles to get back home and the fat one said he hated the thought of riding all that way to North Horsham."

"They're getting really stupid," Nellie said, scowling. "I can't believe we've been imprisoned up here by such a bunch of idiots."

"I still can't believe you helped them get on the base."

"I didn't help them much. I told them about that broken fence post because it's all the way back behind the rec center. If they try getting to the main quarters from there they'll run into the guards."

"Well, we're not going anywhere for a while, so we might as well keep playing 'I Spy.' It will pass the time."

"I hate that game." Nellie yawned. "Besides, it's getting dark. I can't see what you're spying."

"Well, just finish this one. It's a good one, and you don't have to see it to know what it is. It begins with *F*."

Sighing, Nellie tried to concentrate. "Floor?"

"No."

"Fruit."

"There's no fruit in here!"

"How'd you know if we can't see nothing?"

"I know. Now guess again."

Nellie groaned. "I can't. I'm too hungry to think. I give up."

"It's me! Florrie!"

Nellie glared at her. "You can't spy yourself!"

"Why not? I —" Florrie broke off as a faint creak echoed up from below. "What's that?"

"Probably rats," Nellie said gloomily.

Florrie gave a little squeal, then cut it off with a hand over her mouth as another creak was followed by a scraping sound.

Nellie tensed and crept to the edge of the ledge. She could see a thin sliver of light between the doors. "Someone's out there," she whispered.

"They can't be back already," Florrie whispered back. "They only left a few minutes ago."

"Shh!" Nellie shifted closer to the edge. Her eyes widened when she saw one of the doors easing open, an inch at a time. Signaling Florrie to be quiet, she pointed at the door.

Florrie slithered forward on her backside until she could see over the edge.

As they watched, the door opened even wider and a figure slipped through. For a moment or two there was complete silence, then a voice called softly, "Nellie? Florrie? Are you in here?"

"Oh, my God. *Sadie!*" Nellie jumped to her feet, almost sending Florrie over the edge in her excitement. "Up here! We're up here!"

"Thank heavens," Sadie said more loudly. A beam of light from a torch hit Nellie in the face, momentarily blinding her. "What the heck are you doing up there? The whole village has been looking for you two."

"Well, they didn't look very far — that's all I can say. Move that torch off my face. I can't see a bloomin' thing." Nellie dangled her legs over the edge while Florrie jumped up and down making little squealing noises.

"You'd better get down here" — Sadie walked over to where the ladder leaned against the wall — "before them musketeers get back. Where were they going, anyhow?"

"They've gone to the base. And they're not the musketeers. They're just a bunch of silly schoolboys up to no good, that's all."

Sadie dragged the ladder over to the ledge. "Are you telling me little kids trapped you both up there?"

Seeing Sadie's grin, Nellie said hotly, "They're not so little." She'd have said a lot more, except just then the ladder slammed against the ledge, sending up a shower of dust that made them both cough.

"Go on," Nellie said, giving Florrie a little push. "You go first. Make it fast, will you? I don't want to be here when those hooligans get back."

"That's if they come back here." Sadie stood aside and waited for Florrie to climb down. It took her a long time, since she stopped at each rung to feel the next one below her.

Seething with impatience, Nellie waited for her to get to the bottom. "Well, their bicycles are here and they have to get back to North Horsham somehow. Unless they plan on waiting for the bus tomorrow."

"So what are they doing on the base?"

"Dunno, they wouldn't tell us. But they sent a Jeep over the cliff last night and stole another one, so they're not going to just shortsheet the beds, are they. Whatever it is, it's bound to cause some kind of damage."

"We ought to notify the Yanks, then," Sadie said.

Nellie barely waited for Florrie to get clear of the ladder before she scrambled down it. "I don't suppose you've got anything to eat on you?" she asked hopefully.

"Sorry." Sadie hauled the ladder back in place. "I didn't think to bring anything. To be honest, I really didn't think I'd find you."

"How did you know where we were?" Florrie asked, brushing dust and bits of hay from her skirt.

"I was up the top of the windmill, looking out that little window, and I saw this Jeep go tearing across the field. I guessed it was the musketeers — at least we thought they was musketeers — so I watched until they went through the gate and up the lane, then I came looking. This barn was the only place they could have hid someone, so here I am."

"You took a chance, coming out here on your own," Nellie said, impressed at Sadie's bravery.

"I'm not alone. At least, I wasn't." Sadie brushed her hands together, then wiped them on her skirt. "Polly was with me. I don't know what happened, but when I got back down she'd disappeared. I went looking for her, and I thought I heard her scream, but then I went to get my bicycle and hers was gone, so she must have gone back home."

"Probably got scared," Florrie said, nodding. "I don't blame her. I was scared to death. I thought we were going to die."

"We might if we stand around here talking," Nellie said. "Come on, I'm going home. I'm so hungry I could eat a flipping horse."

"Wait a minute." Sadie held up her hand. "By the time we get back to the village and tell the bobbies, we'll probably be too late to stop those boys."

"Probably," Nellie agreed. "Too bad."

"We could wait here for them to get back and capture them."

Nellie stared at her. "Are you crazy? I've been stuck up on the flipping ledge since last night. I'm filthy, I'm dying of thirst, and I'm starving. I'm going home. Let the bobbies catch the buggers."

"I think Nellie's right," Florrie said nervously. "After all, it's not our job to catch them."

Sadie tilted her head to one side and looked at them both in turn. "Don't you want them to pay for what they did to you?"

"Well, of course we want them to pay," Nellie said crossly. "But we know their names and we know they live in North Horsham. It shouldn't be too difficult to find them."

"You know their surnames?"

Nellie sighed. "No, we don't, but —"

"North Horsham's a big town. Do you really think the bobbies are going to waste their time looking for three schoolboys up to mischief?"

"The Yanks will if those chumps do some damage on the base."

"No, they won't," Florrie said. "They'll let the constables take care of it. They got more important things to worry about right now."

"She's right," Sadie said. "Our best chance of catching them is to wait here in the dark for them to get back. There's three of them and three of us. We should be able to take them, right?"

Nellie thought about it long and hard. She wanted nothing more than to eat a plate of fish and chips, drink a gallon of tea, and crawl into her nice, soft bed. On the other hand, it didn't seem right that those bums should get away with all the stuff they put her through. It would feel very, very good to hand them over to the bobbies.

"All right," she said, plopping onto a pile of hay. "Count me in."

Sadie nodded. "Florrie?"

It was too dark to see Florrie's expression, but Nellie could tell she was scared when she said, "Well, I'm not going to walk all the way home in the dark by myself. I suppose I'll have to stay here with you."

"Good for you!" Sadie sat down on the hay next to Nellie.

"How are we going to get them back to Sitting Marsh?" Florrie asked, as she joined the other two on the ground. "They're not going to just walk quietly back with us."

"I thought about that." Sadie didn't sound quite so confident, much to Nellie's dismay. "I'm hoping that Polly will raise the alarm and bring the bobbies back here."

Nellie leaned back against the wall. She had to be crazy to agree to this. There were too many things that could go wrong. They could end up worse off than they were before.

It was too late now, though. She couldn't back out even if she wanted to, or the others would think she was a coward. No, she was the one that had got them all into this; she had to stick it out now. She only hoped that Sadie was right, and that Polly would bring help. She had a nasty feeling they were going to need it.

Chapter 14

Sadie sat with her arms clasped around her knees, her brow furrowed in concentration. "We've got to come up with a plan of attack," she said. "Just in case Polly doesn't come back here with the bobbies." She lifted her head as a thought struck her. "I'm so stupid. If Polly does bring the bobbies back with her, she'll go to the windmill. I should be up there waiting."

"And what if she doesn't?" Nellie demanded. "You'll be at the windmill and we'll be here on our own when those morons get back here."

Sadie thought about it. "All right. Florrie will have to go to the windmill and wait there. You and I will have to tackle the boys."

"Two against three?" Nellie laughed. "That's not giving us much of a chance."

"You said they were only schoolboys."

"They were bloody big schoolboys."

"Bigger than me," Florrie agreed.

"I still say we can do it. After all, we will be surprising them. They think you're up there on the ledge."

"What if we let the air out of their tires?" Florrie suggested. "They wouldn't get very far on their bicycles that way."

"I say we ride their bicycles back to the village," Nellie chimed in. "That's what we should have done in the first place."

"And lose the chance to grab them ourselves?" Sadie laughed. "Just think how they're going to feel when they're captured by women."

"That's if we can capture them." Nellie got up and brushed the straw from her skirt. "I think —"

"Shhh!" Sadie held up her hand. "I hear a Jeep."

"Oh, 'eck," Florrie said, her voice quivering with fright. "They're coming back."

"Well, it looks as if we'll have to do this by ourselves." Sadie got up and brushed her hands together. "Okay, everyone hide. You go over there behind that old tractor, Florrie. You over there, Nellie." She pointed to a pile of hay in the opposite corner. "When I yell *'Now!'* everyone jump out at once."

"And do what?" Florrie asked hoarsely.

"Go for their legs." Sadie positioned herself behind a bale of hay next to the door and switched off the torch. "Get them on the floor and then sit on them."

"What if we can't see their legs?"

"Use your flipping noggin!" Sadie muttered fiercely, just as the noise of the Jeep's engine cut out. She froze, praying the other two wouldn't open their mouths now.

For a long, agonizing moment there was nothing but silence, both inside and outside the barn. Then, slowly, the doors slid open and three figures slipped inside.

"Now!" yelled Sadie. She charged out from behind the bale of hay and slammed into a large body.

"Oof!" said a male voice.

Sadie dropped to her knees and shoved her shoulder hard against her opponent's knees. This time the voice yelled in pain, and went down with a satisfying thump.

Still unable to see clearly, Sadie dumped her backside onto a broad chest. The commotion going on nearby was deafening. Shrieks and screams rent the air, dust flew everywhere, and bodies fell in a tangled mess to the floor.

Then, suddenly, an eerie silence fell over the combatants. The body underneath Sadie didn't move a muscle.

Florrie's voice came out of the dark, high-pitched and shaking. "Sadie?"

Surprised that her opponent had given

up so easily, Sadie said quickly, "You all right, Florrie?"

"Yes." A long pause followed, then Florrie spoke again, in a weird voice Sadie hardly recognized. "But this isn't a boy I'm sitting on."

"Of course not, you blithering idiot," another female voice snapped. "It's me, isn't it."

Hardly able to believe her ears, Sadie turned her head in that direction. "Polly?"

"Yes!" Polly's voice sounded strangled. "Florrie, get off my chest before you suffocate me."

Florrie squealed apologies, amid a lot of scuffling sounds.

"Then who am *I* sitting on?" Nellie demanded.

To Sadie's horror, she heard Lady Elizabeth's hoarse voice answer, "I'm rather afraid it's me."

"Oh, blimey," Nellie muttered.

Sadie briefly closed her eyes. It hadn't been a Jeep at all she'd heard. It must have been her ladyship's motorcycle.

More scuffling followed, with Nellie mumbling over and over, "I'm so terribly sorry, your ladyship. Really I am."

By now Sadie had a really nasty feeling in the pit of her stomach. She shifted her weight and closed her eyes when she heard a groan. "Oh, Gawd," she muttered. "Don't tell me."

"That's George," Polly said, confirming Sadie's worst fears.

Scrambling to her feet, Sadie tried to make the best of it. Flicking on her torch, she said cheerfully, "Well, if you had been the boys, we'd have done a really good job of bringing them down."

"Boys?" Lady Elizabeth sounded bewildered. "What boys?"

"The boys what captured me and Florrie." Quickly Nellie explained.

With heavy grunting, soft cursing, and general thumping, George climbed to his feet. Seconds later, a second bright beam from a torch in his hand swept around the barn.

"Sorry, guv'nor," Sadie said cheerfully. "We thought you was the boys coming back. We were going to capture them and march them back to the village."

"Always supposing they survived your attack," George said dryly. "What do I have to do to get through your heads that it's dangerous to take police matters in your own hands? You all could have been really hurt tackling three thugs like that."

"Well, George," Lady Elizabeth said,

"we have to commend them for trying." She looked a little like a scarecrow with straw sticking out of her hair and clinging to her cardigan. "The thing is, what do we do now?"

"Well, I reckon we wait until they come back." George's voice was doubtful. "If they come back, that is."

"They'll come back for their bicycles," Nellie said. "They're over there by the wall."

George grunted. "Let's hope they bring the Jeep back with them, that's all."

"Wonder what they were up to on the base," Polly said.

"I reckon we're going to find out in a minute." Sadie tilted her head to one side to listen. "Isn't that a Jeep I hear out there?"

"You thought you heard a Jeep just now," Nellie reminded her.

"That was my motorcycle," said Lady Elizabeth. "It does sound awfully like a Jeep at times."

"All right, everybody." George switched off his torch. "Stay out of sight. Nobody move unless I tell you to. Is that clear?"

Feeling somewhat disgruntled at being done out of capturing the hooligans, Sadie turned off her own torch and went back behind her bale of hay. The roar of the Jeep's engine grew steadily louder, then cut off, leaving them all in silence.

Once more the doors slid open, and three shadowy figures filled the doorway. "Just grab the bicycles and get out of here," a gruff voice ordered.

"What about them women up there?" This voice was quite different, soft and whiny.

"Shove the ladder up to the ledge. By the time they get down and walk back to the village we'll be back home."

"What if they tell the bobbies?"

The gruff voice laughed. "So what? Them stupid idiots in Sitting Marsh are too bleeding old and doddery to do anything about it."

"Oh? *Sez who?*"

Sadie jumped as George's voice rang out. Once more the light from his torch lit up the barn, the beam focused on the wide-eyed faces of the boys transfixed in the doorway.

Then, as if jerked by an invisible rope, the three leapt back, turned tail, and ran off into the darkness, with George in hot pursuit.

"Come on!" Sadie yelled. "Don't let them get away!" Turning on her torch again, she charged out into the night air and ran as hard as she could after George, accompanied by pounding feet behind her.

She caught up with him at the gate. He leaned over it, panting for breath, the torch limp in his hand. Seconds later Nellie came up behind them, wheezing like an old bicycle pump.

"They got away," Sadie said, her voice flat with disappointment.

"Went over that gate like they had bloomin' wings," George said breathlessly.

Polly appeared from out of the shadows, breathing hard. "What happened?"

"They're gone," Nellie told her. "We won't catch them now."

"After all that," Sadie added.

"Well, best get back home." George straightened up. "Her ladyship was kind enough to give me a lift on her motorcycle. But seeing as you, Nellie, and Florrie have been through such a terrible experience, I think you should ride back with her ladyship to the village. I'll take one of those bicycles in the barn and the other two women can ride back with me."

"I left my bicycle at the manor," Polly protested.

"You can have one of the boys' bicycles,"

Sadie told her as they trudged back across the field to the barn.

"I can't ride a bicycle with a crossbar," Polly said, sounding really tired.

"Well, then, you can ride mine and I'll ride the boy's one." Sadie linked her arm through her friend's. "How'd you lot know we was in the barn, anyhow?"

"When we got to the windmill and no one was there, George remembered as how one of the farmers told him he kept hearing a Jeep near one of his fields. We saw the barn and decided to have a look, just in case."

"I hope Lady Elizabeth forgives us for knocking her to the ground," Nellie said mournfully.

Sadie chuckled. "She will. She's a good sort. I just wish we could have caught them buggers."

"Too bad they weren't the real musketeers," Nellie said. "Just think if we'd caught *them*. We'd have had our names in the newspapers."

"Well, we couldn't even capture three schoolboys, so I don't think we'd have much chance against the musketeers." Sadie lowered her voice as they reached the barn. "Just be glad it weren't the musketeers. You and Florrie could be dead by now. Like that poor bloke at the wedding."

"Yeah, I'll be glad when whoever did that is caught and in prison."

"Me, too." Sadie shivered. "I just hope we don't meet up with him in the dark on the way home. I think we've all had enough excitement for one night."

"I've had enough to last me a year," Polly murmured. "I think I'll stick to the Tudor Arms for my excitement from now on."

By the time Elizabeth got back to the manor, Violet had already gone to bed. Which was just as well, she told herself as she wearily made her way to the conservatory. Violet tended to get extremely testy when Elizabeth left without telling the housekeeper where she was going.

She badly needed a glass of sherry to settle her nerves. The incident in the barn had upset her more than she was willing to admit. When those bodies had come flying at her out of the dark, she'd been certain they were the musketeers bent on destroying her. Nellie's weight had crushed the air out of her lungs, and for a moment or two she thought she'd taken her last breath.

Predictably, her thoughts had gone immediately to Earl. She'd wondered how long he would mourn her passing, and how soon he would find someone else to take her place. Visions of the brief times they had spent together had flashed through her mind, and she'd been filled with a deep sadness at the thought that she would never be able to enjoy such moments again.

She smiled, wondering what he'd say if he knew how foolish she was where he was concerned. Reaching the door of the conservatory, she pushed it open, then paused in shock.

He was there, lounging in his favorite rocking chair, his head back, his eyes closed.

For a second or two she wondered if she'd conjured up a vision out of her dreams, but then she heard his rhythmic breathing and knew he was really there, sound asleep.

She crept into the room and gently closed the door. A half-empty glass of Scotch sat on the table next to his elbow. In sleep his face looked younger, less tense, his strong jaw relaxed. She had to fight the urge to lean over and kiss his mouth.

They had an agreement, she reminded herself, as she had done so often. Until his divorce was final, they would keep their distance. Or at least try to do so. She smiled again at the memory of the kiss they'd shared on the cliffs . . . was it only a couple of days ago? It seemed like weeks now.

Very carefully she poured herself a glass of sherry and settled down on the white wicker couch. She was prepared to wait all night for him to awaken. He needed his sleep, and the escape that it afforded him from the hell he faced every day.

Only a few minutes passed, however, before his eyelids flickered. She'd heard the change in his breathing and was watching him when he opened his eyes.

His boyish smile warmed her as no fire ever could. "I've died and gone to heaven," he said softly. "There's an angel sitting next to me."

"A rather tarnished angel, I'm afraid," she said, choosing to cover her confusion with her usual dry humor. "What are you doing here?"

"Giving you a nice surprise, I hope." He stretched his arms above his head, presenting her heart with yet more cause to flutter wildly.

"It's a wonderful surprise. I didn't see your Jeep outside."

"The boys dropped me off on their way to the pub."

She found it impossible to remove her gaze from his face. "I was under the impression this morning that you would not be able to get away from the base anytime soon."

"So was I, but our mission was aborted due to the bad weather, so here I am."

"Wonderful." She beamed at him. "How long?"

"Just for tonight. I have to be back in the morning."

Oh, if only she could spend the night with him. The forbidden thought popped into her mind, shocking her to the core. She had never been that kind of person, having been brought up by the strictest of parents.

Her divorce had caused her agonies of embarrassment and had brought shame on her prominent family. She had yet to live that down in the village. She could only imagine the reaction if she should give in to her wanton thoughts. At the same time, she had to marvel at the effect this one man could have on her. Love like this was a powerful thing indeed.

"You're looking very serious," Earl murmured. "Was it something I said?"

She managed a light laugh. "Heavens, no. It's just that I've had rather an exhausting day." She filled him in on the events of the past few hours.

"I was getting a little worried about you," he said, when she was finished. "Violet didn't know you'd gone out. She invited me to wait in here for you, but I could tell she was worried, too." His gaze probed her face. "So the kidnappers disappeared?"

"Yes, I'm afraid so. I would have liked to see them punished for what they did to Nellie and Florrie, and then there's that Jeep they destroyed on the beach. We still don't know what damage they did at the base."

"I'll probably find out tomorrow," Earl said, sounding grim. "What about the murder case? How's that coming?"

Elizabeth sighed. "It's complicated. False leads, mixed signals, not much evidence to go on . . . I'm really no closer than I was at the beginning."

"I guess the constables aren't much help, either."

"Your guess is right. I do have one more person I want to talk to tomorrow. Other than that, I really don't know what to think."

"Well, I really don't want to waste my one night at home talking about murder and other unpleasant things." He smiled at her so sweetly her heart ached. "Tell me what you were like when you were little."

"Precocious."

He laughed. "I figured that." He took a sip of his Scotch and put it down. "No, really. Tell me. I want to know."

"I'll tell if you tell me what you were like as a little boy."

His grin widened. "You've got a deal."

She settled back to enjoy what she knew was going to be a fascinating conversation. If only she could go on like this forever — sitting so close to him, listening to his deep voice, getting to know him, watching the laughter light up his blue eyes, and feeling as if she were seventeen once more and so madly, madly in love.

It was late when she finally said good night to him. She could tell he wanted to kiss her. She had never wanted anything more in her life, but she knew once they gave in to the temptation, others would follow. That path was too dangerous; it was still too soon.

She lay awake for a long time thinking about him and their nebulous future. She'd tried to avoid as much as possible thinking about what would happen to them when the war eventually ended. He would be sent back to America, of course.

Would he ask her to go back with him? Could she go if he did? Those two questions were unanswerable. She could only hold on to what they had now, watching the days slip away, waiting for his divorce to become final.

What if the war ended before that happened? What if he had to go back a married man? Would they ever be free to love as she so desperately wanted? Was she being a fool clinging to protocol, wasting what little time she could have with him with her vague fears of further besmirching her tremulous reputation?

Perhaps, but her values and heritage were impossible to ignore. She flung herself over onto her side and buried her face in the pillow. She had to stop tormenting herself with her doubts. Her emotions were at war with her morals, and there wasn't much she could do about it. Sooner or later she would have to face the inevitable, and one or the other would win. It was only a matter of time.

She could either abandon her legacy and all it stood for to follow the man she loved halfway across the world, or wallow in regrets for what she had missed for the rest of her life. Only she could make that decision. When the time was right. Until then, all she could do was pray that whatever she decided, she would choose the right path.

For both of them.

Chapter 15

Earl had already left when Elizabeth went down to the kitchen the next morning. Violet told her he had stopped in to say good-bye, and that he hadn't wanted to wake her.

Elizabeth wasn't sure if she was relieved or disappointed. She always avoided actually saying good-bye to him, yet she bitterly resented losing the chance to see him, if only for a minute or two. She ate her breakfast in silence, trying to ignore her housekeeper's attempts to find out where she'd gone the night before.

Martin, as usual, was hidden behind the newspaper, making little tsking noises whenever he saw something that upset him.

Violet's patience finally gave out as Elizabeth was finishing her second cup of tea. "I don't know why we have to have so many secrets in this house," she muttered. "All I ask is that you let me know when you're leaving, Lizzie, so I don't have to worry about you. Remember how you worried about me when you didn't know where I was."

"If I'd told you where I was going," Elizabeth said mildly, "you'd have worried even more."

Violet spun around to stare at her. "I knew it! You went after that murderer, didn't you."

The newspaper rattled as Martin lowered it. "Murderer? What murderer? Don't tell me someone else has been killed."

"It's the same one, you nitwit," Violet snapped. "The man they found in the cellar at the wedding."

"What was he doing in the cellar in the first place, that's what I want to know." He peered at Elizabeth over the top of his glasses. "They don't have any wine down there, you know."

"How'd you know that?" Violet demanded. "You've never been down there. How'd you know what they have or don't have?"

"Someone told me." Martin lifted the newspaper again and disappeared behind it.

Elizabeth and Violet exchanged glances. "Who told you that, Martin?" Elizabeth inquired.

"I don't know, madam. Some young fellow in the kitchen. I didn't catch his name."

"Why did he tell you there was no wine in the cellar?"

Martin lowered the newspaper again. "Because I asked him if there was any down there, madam. I don't like champagne. Nasty stuff. The bubbles fly up my nose and make my eyes water. Most unbecoming and quite embarrassing."

"They had scrumpy, too," Violet reminded him.

Martin gave her a withering look. "I don't care to imbibe an obnoxious liquid that has been produced by fermenting sour apples."

"Where do you think wine comes from then?" Violet demanded.

"Wine is made from grapes, as any fool should know."

"Well, then."

Martin sniffed. "Grapes are far superior to apples."

"They're still fermented fruit, aren't they? It's just a different color, that's all."

Martin sat in silence for a moment, then he shook the paper before lifting it in front of his face. "One might have expected a ludicrous comment like that from such an unenlightened cretin," he murmured.

"Here, what do you mean by that?" Violet looked at Elizabeth for help.

Hoping to spare her housekeeper's feelings, Elizabeth declined to answer.

Unfortunately, Martin had no such scruples. "Cretin," he repeated. "I believe in the more popular vernacular, the word is 'nitwit.' "

Violet opened her mouth to protest, but Elizabeth forestalled her. "Martin, when were you in the kitchen asking for wine?"

"At the wedding, madam."

"Yes, Martin. I understand that. I meant about what time was it?"

"I didn't look at the clock. It was when those silly women were making such a fuss about the knife to cut the wedding cake." Martin shook the newspaper then turned the page. "I was looking for something to drink with my food. It's not good for the digestion, to eat without drinking something. All I could see was champagne and that disgusting cider, so I went into the kitchen to see if they had a bottle of wine."

"And that's when you saw the gentleman?"

"Yes, madam."

"What was he doing?"

Martin gave her a puzzled look. "Doing?"

"Well, was he just standing there, was he by the cellar door, was he at the sink?"

"Actually, madam, he was on his way out. He seemed in rather a hurry. He was quite abrupt when I asked him about the wine. I apologized for bothering him and said I would look in the cellar for a bottle, but he became quite agitated. He was most emphatic about there not being any wine down there. He actually escorted me out of that kitchen, rather rudely in my opinion. I had to settle for some insipid tea that the bakery woman had made earlier. The most I can say for that is that it was wet."

Elizabeth barely heard his last comments. "This gentleman. Was he tall, rather stout, with graying hair?"

Martin nodded. "Yes, madam. That's the chap. I think he was with the leggy bridesmaid. Good-looking woman, for her age."

Violet huffed out her breath but Elizabeth ignored her. "Of course," she said softly. "I should have known."

Martin looked confused. "I beg your pardon?"

"Never mind." Elizabeth got up from the table. "Violet, I'm going to Priscilla's flat. I have the proofs from the wedding and I need to drop them off there."

Martin began struggling to his feet, muttering something under his breath.

"Can't I see them first?" Violet wiped her hands on her apron. "If I remember rightly, I had a nice one taken with Charlie."

Elizabeth stared at her, intrigued to see her housekeeper blushing. "Why, Violet, I do believe you're beginning to care for Charlie Gibbons. Are you going out with him again?"

Violet did her best to appear unconcerned, but the fluttering of her hands gave her away. "As a matter of fact, Mr. Gibbons is thinking of moving to Sitting Marsh. He likes the village and the people here, and it will mean he'll be close to his brother and his new sister-in-law."

Elizabeth smiled. "How nice for you, Violet. It's about time you had a gentleman friend. Everyone needs someone to care for and cherish."

Martin, who had finally steadied himself on his feet, sniffed. "Now, I suppose, we shall have to listen to a lot of sentimental drivel about gentleman friends and clandestine rendezvous."

"Better than listening to you bleat about your lottery lady," Violet snapped.

Fortunately the telephone rang, putting an end to what might have been a lengthy argument. Violet picked up the telephone and spoke into it.

Elizabeth waited, hoping against hope, yet afraid to expect too much.

Violet pulled the receiver away from her

ear and looked at her. "It's your major."

Fighting to hide her apprehension, Elizabeth took the telephone and murmured a breathless, "Earl? Is everything all right?"

His rich voice reassured her. "Everything's fine. I just thought you'd like to know what your kidnappers were up to at the base last night."

"Oh, dear." Elizabeth pressed the receiver to her ear and tried to forget there were others in the room. "I hope they didn't do too much damage."

"They burned down the rec room. According to the note they left, their girlfriends had abandoned them in favor of GIs, and they weren't too happy about it."

"Oh, Lord. I am so sorry, Earl. Is it at all salvageable?"

"Not much of it. We'll have to rebuild. The guys are going to miss that place. Those little thugs couldn't have picked a better payback."

"It's a shame. Nobody deserved that."

"There's something else you need to know."

Something in his voice warned her. "What is it?"

"There's some heavy hush-hush meetings going on. Everyone's being confined to the base. It may be a week or so before I can leave."

She swallowed. "Is it the invasion?"

"Elizabeth —"

"I know, you can't tell me. I shouldn't have asked."

"I'll be back just as soon as I can. You know that."

"Yes, I do." She pulled in her breath. "God speed, Earl. Take care of yourself."

"I'll be fine. I'm still carrying your scarf, by the way. The one you gave me when I left last year. It goes everywhere with me."

Somehow she wasn't consoled by that. It was the first time he'd mentioned it since he'd been back. It sounded like an omen. "I'm glad to hear that. I pray it will keep you safe."

"It has so far." He lowered his voice. "I have to go. I'll call when I can."

She nodded, even though he couldn't see her. Unable to trust her voice for more than a couple of words, she said quickly, "Till we meet again."

"So long, sweetheart."

She replaced the receiver, already feeling the loss. "Don't hold off lunch for me," she told Violet, as she headed for the door. "I might be late. I'll bring back some fish and chips."

"Fish and chips!"

Martin looked so hopeful she had to smile. "All right, I'll bring them back for all of us. Though you might have to wait a bit longer. The girls might not like that."

"The girls are servants, madam. They'll do as they're told."

"Don't tell them that." Elizabeth reached the door and opened it. "Polly informed me that domestics, as they are now called, don't like being referred to as servants."

"It was good enough for their forefathers, it's good enough for them today."

"I'm afraid not, Martin." Elizabeth sent him an affectionate smile. "The world is changing, whether we like it or not. We will have to change with it."

Martin drew himself up as straight as his bowed shoulders allowed. "Never! There will always be an England, as long as we defend her shores and carry on her traditions!"

"Oh, Gawd, now he'll start caterwauling," Violet muttered, giving him a dirty look.

Elizabeth closed the door behind her, her smile fading. Traditions. How many was she breaking with her passion for Earl Monroe? How many more would she break before it was over? It was something she couldn't think about now.

She hurried outside, disheartened by the sight of a clear blue sky. Once she had loved the good weather, so rare in that part of the country. But that was before the war. Before clear skies allowed airplanes to fly, taking courageous young men into danger and, far too often, to their deaths.

Astride her motorcycle, she roared down the hill to the High Street. Pulling up outside the police station, she was relieved to see George and Sid's bicycles leaning against the wall. She had made a promise to Earl, and this time she would keep it.

She found George at his desk as usual and quickly explained why she needed him with her.

"Right," he said, when she was finished. Raising his voice, he called out, "Sid, take over here. I have some business to take care of with her ladyship."

"You found the boys that burned down the Yanks' gym?" Sid asked, as he emerged from the back room.

"I'm afraid not." Elizabeth exchanged glances with George. "They are somewhere in North Horsham, I presume. I'm sure you'll catch up with them sooner or later."

"I doubt it," George said, as he pulled

on his helmet. "The case has been taken over by the North Horsham constabulary. It seems the Americans put in a rather strong complaint."

"One can hardly blame them," Elizabeth murmured. She waited for George to open the door for her, then hurried outside to her motorcycle. "Can you manage to squeeze yourself into the sidecar again?" she asked as George approached.

"Not on your life, your ladyship. I'll be quite happy on my bicycle, thank you."

"But we will get there so much more quickly."

"I'll manage very well on my own. Thank you, m'm." George walked over to his bicycle and bent over to fasten a clip around each ankle. "I'll be right behind you when you get there. You'll see."

Seriously doubting that, Elizabeth had to give in gracefully. She rode slowly down to the Tudor Arms. Even so, by the time she arrived there George was nowhere to be seen. Impatient now, she rang the bell on the back door and waited for Alfie to open it.

His bushy eyebrows shot up at the sight of her. "Lady Elizabeth! Whatever . . . ?"

"I'd like a word with Malcolm," she said, giving him no time to form the question. "Is he here?"

"Afraid you've just missed him." Curiosity was written all over his face, but he knew better than to ask. "I do believe he's on his way to see his lady friend, Fiona."

"Thank you, Alfie." Elizabeth turned away, then added over her shoulder, "Oh, when George turns up, tell him where I've gone, will you?"

"George is coming here?"

Hearing his bewilderment, she wished she had time to explain. "He's following me," she said, climbing back onto her motorcycle. "Do tell him to hurry, won't you?" She roared off, drowning out whatever Alfie was saying.

It took her several minutes to reach the flat. Priscilla lived above the ironmongery and normally the shop would have been busy. However, since the war had taken many of the men who purchased the tools and gardening implements, business was no longer brisk. Which suited Elizabeth. She did not need a large audience to witness her visit, or the outcome.

Fiona opened the door to her knock, obviously taken aback by the lady of the manor's second visit in as many days. Again she seemed reluctant to allow Elizabeth to enter, but was left with no choice when her guest deliberately walked through the door and into the cramped front room.

At least the room looked more tidy than when she'd last visited, Elizabeth observed. Malcolm Ludwick sat on the couch, reading a newspaper. He leapt to his feet when Elizabeth walked in, and his expression was not too welcoming. He greeted her in a surly tone of voice and offered her a seat.

Hoping fervently that George wasn't too far behind, Elizabeth sat on the couch. "I quite forgot the reason for my visit yesterday," she said, as Fiona perched on the arm of the chair that Malcolm now occupied. "I had the proofs of the wedding with me, and I meant to leave them with you. I'm afraid I'm becoming quite scatterbrained lately." She drew the packet from her handbag and handed them to Fiona. "They are quite lovely. I'm sure Priscilla will be most pleased. Have you heard from her, by the way?"

"Not yet, your ladyship. There hasn't been enough time for a postcard to reach us from Scotland." Fiona took out the proofs and started thumbing through them.

"Oh, of course not." Elizabeth laughed. "How silly of me. It seems much longer since she and Wally went on their honeymoon. Time drags so much these days. I suppose we're all waiting for the Allied invasion to take place. One rather hopes that it will end the war, though I suppose that's wishful thinking for the most part."

She smiled at Malcolm and felt a chill when she saw his narrowed gaze on her face.

"Well, thank you very much, your ladyship." Fiona stood up, the proofs still in her hand. "I appreciate you bringing these over. Priscilla will be thrilled to find them waiting for her when she gets home."

"I imagine they are having a marvelous time in Scotland," Elizabeth said, leaning back on the couch. "Although the weather can be quite beastly this time of year. I do think they might have done better to have gone to Somerset or Cornwall. So much warmer down there."

Fiona seemed at a loss what to do next. She glanced at Malcolm, who still had his gaze pinned on Elizabeth's face. "Er . . . I suppose I should offer you a cup of tea," she said, making it clear it was the last thing she wanted to do.

"Oh, that sounds lovely!" Elizabeth glanced at the small clock on the mantelpiece. *Where the devil was George?* He should have been here by now.

"Actually, we were just on the way out," Malcolm said, getting to his feet. "So if you would excuse us, your ladyship —"

"Of course." Elizabeth made no effort to move. "I'm so glad you are here, Mr. Ludwick. Before you go, I have a question I'd like to ask you."

She could see it in his eyes. The guilt, underlined with fear. She'd seen that look before. The question was, could she get him to confess what he'd done?

He pretended to be puzzled, though she was quite sure he knew what she was talking about. "Question?"

"Yes." She smiled at him. She could only stall for so long. If George didn't get there very soon, she could be walking into trouble again. Earl would not like that. "When George talked to you at the wedding —"

"Excuse me," he interrupted. "George?"

"Yes." Elizabeth met his gaze. "Police Constable George Dalrymple."

She saw the muscles in his jaw tighten. "Oh, yes, I think I remember. Bald-headed chap. Bit of a bumbler."

Elizabeth smiled. "I suppose he is, at times. Anyway, I seem to remember you telling him that you overheard Tess Winterhalter arguing with the deceased that afternoon. Furious with him, I believe you said?"

Malcolm appeared reluctant to answer, and Fiona answered for him. "That's right, Malcolm. I heard you say that. I remember being surprised that you knew —"

"Shut up!" Malcolm snarled.

Fiona reared back as if she'd been struck, one hand at her mouth.

Elizabeth saw the dawning realization in the woman's eyes and felt sorry for her. Turning back to Malcolm, she said quietly, "You overheard Tess accusing him of taking Fiona to his room, didn't you? You probably saw her threaten him with the knife then lock him in the cellar. Maybe the idea came to you then. Here was your chance to get rid of your rival and blame it on the young girl who was so angry with her boyfriend."

Malcolm apparently was prepared to bluff his way out. "Utter poppycock! I barely knew the chap. As for him being a rival, that's utter nonsense."

"Is it?" Elizabeth smiled. "I think not. Fiona is a woman of means, and you weren't about to lose your benefactor to a two-faced schemer like Brian Sutcliffe. When you heard that Fiona had been to his room, you were afraid he'd charm her away from you. You were presented with a chance to solve that problem and you took it."

Fiona gasped. "No! I don't believe it!"

"Good," Malcolm said roughly. "Because it isn't true. Yes, I heard the bridesmaid arguing with Sutcliffe, but I left right away. Didn't want to embarrass the girl. I never went back into the kitchen after that."

"What were you doing there in the first place?"

"I was getting Fiona a glass of water."

"That's right," Fiona said quickly. "I was thirsty and wanted some water."

Elizabeth nodded. "And you never went back to the kitchen after that?"

"No, of course I didn't."

She glanced at the clock again. George had to be close by now. "That's strange. My butler told me he met you in the kitchen. Apparently he was looking for wine and you told him there was none in the cellar."

The icy calm that crept into his eyes unsettled her. "That's right, I remember now. I met him on the way out."

"But that had to be later. Martin said you were alone, which meant Tess had already left the kitchen."

"Perhaps it was. I don't remember." He turned and grasped Fiona's arm, so tightly she let out a gasp of pain. "Now, if you'll excuse us, your ladyship, we really do have to leave."

"I'm just curious, Mr. Ludwick. How did you know there was no wine in the cellar?"

Fiona tugged at her arm, but instead of letting go, he held her tighter, making her wince. "I didn't," he said shortly. "I told the old boy that because I was afraid he'd go looking for wine and fall and hurt himself."

Elizabeth got slowly to her feet. "I don't think so," she said firmly. "I think you went back later, thinking that Brian Sutcliffe was still locked in the cellar. You found the door was open and went in to investigate. I believe you found him at the foot of the stairs, having fallen, perhaps unconscious. You saw the knife and stabbed him with it. Then you left. You told Martin there was no wine down there to get rid of him. You couldn't have him finding the body while you were still there. It was too risky."

Malcolm was smiling, but there was no humor in it at all. "Very clever, Lady Elizabeth. Unfortunately for you, no one will ever hear that theory."

"Malcolm!" Fiona cried. "What are you going to do?"

"I'm going to get rid of her." He backed toward the door, dragging Fiona with him. He reached with his free hand into his pocket and withdrew a cigarette lighter. He flicked the wheel with his thumb, while Fiona gasped in horror.

"No! I won't let you do this!"

"You don't have any say in it." Malcolm reached the door. "This place is old. It will go up like a bonfire. Too bad Lady Elizabeth was trapped inside when the place burned down." He held the flickering flame to the newspaper lying on the hallstand. It immediately burst into hungry flames that quickly ate up the pages.

Fiona screamed, and Elizabeth stepped forward. "Let her go!"

"Not on your life. I've killed for her now and she's going to keep me in comfort for the rest of my life."

"No, I'm not!" Fiona screamed. "I hate you! I'll see you hang first."

"I don't think so, my dear." Again Malcolm's mouth stretched in an evil grin. "If you want to live, you'll do exactly what I say. If you breathe a word about what happened here, or what was said here, I'll make sure you share the same fate as our esteemed lady of the manor."

The flames were now devouring the coats and scarves on the hallstand, and the smoke curled up to the ceiling. Elizabeth coughed and started toward the door. She never saw Malcolm's fist coming. All she saw were stars, as a jolting pain shot through her jaw and her knees buckled under her. From a distance she heard Fiona scream again, then everything faded into black.

Elizabeth opened her eyes and blinked. She lay on a couch in an unfamiliar room, and people milled around, all seemingly talking at once.

"She's awake!" said a gruff voice, and then George was bending over her, his red-rimmed eyes full of concern. All right, your ladyship?"

Elizabeth coughed and sat up, feeling immensely uncomfortable. She recognized Arnold, the elderly ironmonger, and his wife Trudy, who was hovering at her husband's elbow, her face taut with anxiety.

"I'm quite all right," Elizabeth assured them, surprised to hear her voice so hoarse. Actually she felt rather dizzy, but she wasn't about to admit that. "What happened?"

"I got there just in time to see Ludwick dragging Mrs. Farnsworth out of the burning flat," George told her. "I hit him with my truncheon and he went down like a wounded pheasant. Mrs. Farnsworth told me everything. Luckily the fire hadn't got much of a hold. Arnold and some of the other shopkeepers managed to put it out. The fire brigade is on the way to make sure everything's under control. I'm afraid the new bride will be coming back to a bit of a mess, though."

"What about Fiona?" Elizabeth swung her feet to the ground. "Is she all right?"

"She's at the station, helping Sid write out a report. The inspector's on his way to take Ludwick into custody. Right now he's locked up in our cell."

Very carefully, Elizabeth got to her feet. She had to hang onto the arm of the couch to steady herself, but gradually the room stopped swimming around.

"I wouldn't do that, if I were you, your ladyship," George said, looking anxious. "Trudy here rang the doctor. He's on his way to look you over."

"Oh, I wish you hadn't bothered him." Elizabeth smiled at Trudy. "I'm sure some fresh air is all I need." She started coughing again and Trudy hurried forward.

"Come with me, your ladyship, into the back garden. You're right, you need some fresh air. You can wait for the doctor out there. I have a nice comfortable deck chair you can sit on until he gets here."

She refused to take no for an answer, and Elizabeth allowed herself to be led outside onto a pleasant square of lawn where Trudy settled her onto a deck chair.

"There," said the ironmonger's wife, as she handed Elizabeth a copy of *Woman's Weekly.* "You just rest there and I'll bring you a nice cup of tea. I'm sure the doctor will be here in no time."

Thanking her, Elizabeth made herself more comfortable on the chair. Perhaps she was just a little tired. She couldn't help wondering what Earl would say when he heard about her narrow escape. Perhaps it was foolish to go into Priscilla's flat without George. Then again, they might never have got a confession from the man if George had been there. So it all worked out, after all.

A faint drone in the distance drew her attention to the sky. Airplanes. She shaded her eyes against the bright sunlight, and finally she could see them — a huge formation of bombers flying low toward the coast.

They drew closer, the leading formation almost overhead. She could see the markings on their wings. The distinctive white star on the blue circle confirmed her fears. American airplanes. Earl must be up there somewhere with them.

She watched them until they disappeared from sight, the drone of their engines fading into silence. Someday she would not have to watch like this, her heart full of fear for him and his men. Someday the war would end, and all this agony of uncertainty and despair would be over.

Someday.

She could only hope that day would come soon.

We hope you have enjoyed this Large Print book. Other Thorndike, Wheeler or Chivers Press Large Print books are available at your library or directly from the publishers.

For more information about current and upcoming titles, please call or write, without obligation, to:

Publisher
Thorndike Press
295 Kennedy Memorial Drive
Waterville, ME   04901
Tel. (800) 223-1244

Or visit our Web site at:
www.gale.com/thorndike
www.gale.com/wheeler

OR

Chivers Large Print
published by BBC Audiobooks Ltd
St James House, The Square
Lower Bristol Road
Bath BA2 3BH
England
Tel. +44(0) 800 136919
email: bbcaudiobooks@bbc.co.uk
www.bbcaudiobooks.co.uk

All our Large Print titles are designed for easy reading, and all our books are made to last.